frozen charlotte

frozen charlotte

ALEX BELL

SCHOLASTIC PRESS | NEW YORK

Text copyright © 2014 by Alex Bell
Extract from *Sleepless* © 2014 by Lou Morgan

Library of Congress Cataloging-in-Publication Data available

ISBN 978-0-545-94108-2

10 9 8 7 6 5 4 3 2 1   16 17 18 19 20

Printed in the U.S.A. 23

First American edition, December 2016

Book design by Carol Ly

FOR MY MOST GORGEOUS COUSIN,
GEORGIANA MAUNDER-WILLRICH—
FRIEND, ROOMMATE, CINEMA BUDDY, ROLLER
COASTER PAL, AND HONORARY SISTER.

ISLE OF SKYE—1910

The girls were playing with the Frozen Charlotte dolls again.

The schoolmistress had given them some scraps of fabric and ribbon from the sewing room to take out to the garden. They were to practice their embroidery skills by making little dresses and bonnets for the naked porcelain dolls. "They'll catch their death of cold otherwise," the teacher had said.

But there was one girl who wasn't playing with the others. The schoolmistress sighed when she saw her, sitting alone, fiddling with her blindfold. The girl complained it was uncomfortable but the doctor had said it was necessary to keep her wound clean. And, besides, the sight of her ruined eyes frightened the other girls.

The schoolmistress got up and went over to her, just as she succeeded in untying the knot.

"Now, Martha," she said, deftly tying it back up again. "Remember what the doctor said."

The girl hung her head and said nothing. She hadn't spoken much since the accident. Not since the doctor had come and Martha had made those ridiculous accusations.

"Why don't you go and join the girls in their game?" the schoolmistress said.

The blind girl shook her head and spoke so quietly that the teacher had to strain to hear. "It's a bad game."

"Nonsense. Come along now and play with the others. I'm sure they can help you if you ask."

She took Martha's hand and tugged her, stumbling along, to where the girls were playing in the sunshine. But when she got there she found that they weren't making dresses for the dolls after all. They were making shrouds. And they'd covered the dolls up with them as if they were corpses. Some of the girls were even making little crosses out of twigs.

"What are you doing?" the schoolmistress said.

The girls looked up at her. "We're holding a funeral for the Frozen Charlottes, Miss Grayson."

"Well, stop it at once," the teacher replied. "I never heard of anything so ghoulish."

"But, miss," one of the girls said, "they like being dead. They told us."

ONE

Now Charlotte lived on the mountainside,
In a bleak and dreary spot.
There was no house for miles around,
Except her father's cot.

When Jay said he'd downloaded a Ouija-board app on to his phone, I wasn't surprised. It sounded like the kind of crazy thing he'd do. It was Thursday night and we were sitting in our favorite greasy spoon café, eating baskets of curly fries, like always.

"Do we have to do this?" I asked.

"Yes. Don't be a spoilsport," Jay said.

He put his phone on the table and loaded the app. A Ouija board filled the screen. The words YES and NO were written in flowing script in the top two corners, and beneath them were the letters of the alphabet in that same curling text, in two arches. Beneath that was a straight row of numbers from zero to nine, and underneath was printed GOOD BYE.

"Isn't there some kind of law against Ouija boards or something? I thought they were supposed to be dangerous."

"Dangerous how? It's only a board with some letters and numbers written on it."

"I heard they were banned in England."

"Couldn't be, or they wouldn't have made the app. You're not scared, are you? It's only a bit of fun."

"I am definitely *not* scared," I said.

"Hold your hand over the screen then."

So I held out my hand, and Jay did the same, our fingertips just touching.

"The planchette thing is supposed to spell out the answers to our questions," Jay said, indicating the little pointed disc hovering at one corner of the screen.

"Without us even touching it?"

"The ghost will move it," he declared.

"A ghost that understands cell phones? And doesn't mind crowds?" I glanced around the packed café. "I thought you were supposed to play with Ouija boards in haunted houses and abandoned train stations."

"That would be pretty awesome, Sophie, but since we don't have any boarded-up lunatic asylums or whatever around here, we'll just have to make do with what we've got. Who shall we try to contact?" Jay asked. "Jack the Ripper? Mad King George? The Birdman of Alcatraz?"

"Rebecca Craig," I said. The name came out without my really meaning it to.

"Never heard of her. Who did she kill?"

"No one. She's my dead cousin."

Jay raised an eyebrow. "Your what?"

"My uncle who lives in Scotland, he used to have another daughter, but she died when she was seven."

"How?"

I shrugged. "I don't know. No one really talks about it. It was some kind of accident."

"How well did you know her?"

"Not that well. I only met her once. It must have been right before she died. But I always wondered how it happened. And I guess I've just been thinking about them again, now that I'm going to stay there over vacation."

"Okay, let's ask her how she died. Rebecca Craig," Jay said. "We invite you to speak with us."

Nothing happened.

"Rebecca Craig," Jay said again. "Are you there?"

"It's not going to work," I said. "I told you we should have gone to a haunted house."

"Why don't *you* try calling her?" Jay said. "Perhaps she'll respond to you better. You're family, after all."

I looked down at the Ouija board and the motionless planchette. "Rebecca Craig—"

I didn't even finish the sentence before the disc started

5

to move. It glided smoothly once around the board before coming back to hover where it had been before.

"Is that how spirits say hello, or just the app glitching out?" I asked.

"Shh! You're going to upset the board with your negativity. Rebecca Craig," Jay said again. "Is that you? Your cousin would like to speak with you."

"We're not technically—" I began, but the planchette was already moving. Slowly it slid over to YES, and then quickly returned to the corner of the board.

"It's obviously got voice-activation software," I said. With my free hand I reached across the table to steal one of Jay's fries.

He tsk-tsked at me, then said, "Spirit, how did you die?" The planchette hovered a little longer this time before sliding over towards the letters and spelling out: B-L-A-C-K

"What's that supposed to mean?" I asked.

"It's not finished," Jay replied.

The planchette went on to spell: S-A-N-D

"Black sand?" I said. "That's a new one. Maybe she meant to say quicksand? Do they have quicksand in Scotland?"

"Spirit," Jay began, but the planchette was already moving again. One by one, it spelled out seven words: D-A-D-D-Y

S-A-Y-S

N-E-V-E-R

E-V-E-R

O-P-E-N

T-H-E

G-A-T-E

"It's like a Magic 8 Ball," I said. "It just comes out with something random each time."

"Shh! It's not random, we're speaking with the dead," Jay said, somehow managing to keep a straight face, even when I stuck my tongue out at him. "Is that why you died, spirit?" he asked. "Because you opened the gate?"

The planchette started to move again, gliding smoothly around the lighted screen:

C-H-A-R-L-O-T-T-E

I-S

C-O-L-D

"Charlotte?" I said. "I thought we were speaking to Rebecca?"

"Is your name Charlotte?" Jay asked.

The planchette moved straight to NO.

"Are you Rebecca Craig?" I asked.

The planchette did a little jump before whizzing over to YES. And then:

C-H-A-R-L-O-T-T-E

I-S

C-O-L-D

C-O-L-D

C-H-A-R-L-O-T-T-E

I-S

C-O-L-D

C-H-A-R-L-O-T-T-E

I-S

C-O-L-D

"This ghost has a pretty one-track mind," I said with a yawn. "I hope you didn't pay a lot of money for this rubbish. Aren't you supposed to be saving up for a new bike?"

"Yes, but I hate saving money—it's so boring. Maybe I'll get a unicycle instead. Do you think that would make me more popular at school?"

I laughed. "Only if you went to clown school. You'd fit right in there. Probably make Head Boy."

"Head Boy, wouldn't that be something? My mom would die of pride." Jay looked down at the board and said, "You know, some people think that spirits can see into the future. Let's give it a little test. Rebecca, am I ever going to grow another couple of inches taller?"

I giggled as the planchette whizzed around, apparently at random.

N-E-V-E-R

E-V-E-R

O-P-E-N

T-H-E

G-A-T-E

D-A-D-D-Y

S-A-Y-S

D-A-D-D-Y

S-A-Y-S

T-I I-E

G-A-T-E

N-E-V-E-R

E-V-E-R

"Do you think I should take that as a no?" Jay asked me.

"Absolutely. Short for life."

Jay pretended to recoil. "Geez, you don't have to be vicious about it." He looked back down at the board. "Spirit, am I going to pass that math quiz tomorrow?"

B-L-A-C-K

S-A-N-D

F-R-O-Z-E-N

C-H-A-R-L-O-T-T-E

F-R-O-Z-E-N

S-A-N-D

B-L-A-C-K

C-H-A-R-L-O-T-T-E

C-O-L-D

H-E-R-E

D-A-D-D-Y

Jay and I were both giggling now, like little kids, but his next, and final, question made the laugh stick in my throat. "When will I die?"

This time the planchette gave a different answer. It whizzed around the board aimlessly once again before clearly spelling out seven letters:

T-O-N-I-G-H-T

"I don't think this ghost likes me very much," Jay said, lifting his eyes to mine. "What do you think?"

But before I could respond, we both jumped as a tinkly, music-box style tune started to play from Jay's phone.

"Is that your new ringtone?" I asked.

"I've never heard it before," Jay replied.

"Now you're just messing with me."

He shook his head and gave me his best innocent look. "It must be part of the app. To make it more spooky."

A girl's voice started to sing—plaintive and childish, high-pitched and wobbly. It was a simple, lilting melody full of melancholy, a song made for quiet campfires, lonely hills, and cold nights:

Now Charlotte lived on the mountainside,
In a bleak and dreary spot.

There was no house for miles around,
Except her father's cot.

"You are such a wind-up," I said, smiling and giving Jay's arm a shove. The singsong voice was starting to get us dirty looks from the other customers in the café. "You put that on there yourself!"

"I swear I didn't," Jay replied. "It's just a really cool app."

Such a dreadful night I never saw,
The reins I scarce can hold.
Fair Charlotte shivering faintly said,
"I am exceedingly cold."

Jay tapped the screen to turn it off but, though the voice stopped singing, the Ouija board screen wouldn't close. The planchette started spinning around the board manically.

"Dude, I think that app has broken your phone," I said.

It was only a joke. I didn't really think there was anything wrong with the phone that turning it off and on again wouldn't fix, but then the screen light started to flicker, and all the lights in the café flickered with it.

Jay and I looked at each other and I saw the first glimmer of uncertainty pass over his face.

And then every light in the café went out, leaving us in total darkness.

There were grumblings and mutterings from the other customers around us and, somewhere in the room, a small child started to cry. We heard the loud crash of something being dropped in the kitchen.

The only light in the room came from the glow of Jay's phone, still on the table between us. I looked at it and saw the planchette fly over to number nine and then start counting down through the numbers. When it got to zero, someone in the café screamed, a high, piercing screech that went on and on.

Cold, clammy fingers curled around mine as Jay took my hand in the darkness and squeezed it tight. I could hear chairs scraping on the floor as people stood up, demanding to know what was happening. More children started to cry, and I could hear glasses and things breaking as people tried to move around in the dark and ended up bumping into tables. And above it all was the piercing sound of a woman crying hysterically, as if something really awful was happening to her.

I let go of Jay's hand and twisted around in my seat, straining my eyes, peering into the darkness, desperately trying to make sense of what was happening. Now that my eyes had adjusted, I could just make out the silhouettes of some of the other people in the café with us—plain black shapes, like shadow puppets dancing on a wall.

But one of them was taller than all the others, impossibly tall, and I realized that whoever it was must be standing on one of the tables. They weren't moving, not at all. Everyone else in the café was moving, even if only turning their heads this way and that, but this person stood stock-still. I couldn't even tell if I was looking at their back or their front—they were just staring straight ahead, arms by their sides.

"Do you see that?" I said, but my voice got lost amongst all the others. I stood up and took half a step forward, staring through the shadows. I could just make out the outline of long hair and a skirt. It was a girl standing on the table in the middle of all this chaos. No one else seemed to have noticed her.

"Jay—" I began, turning back towards him at the exact moment his phone died. The screen light flickered and then went off. At the same time, the café lights came back on. I spun back around to look at the table where the girl had been standing, but there was no one there. The table was empty.

"Did you see her?" I asked Jay.

"See who?"

I stared around for the girl in a skirt, but there was no sign of her.

Anyone would think there'd been an earthquake or something. There was broken china and glass all over the floor of the café, many of the chairs had fallen over, and a couple of tables had overturned.

"Who was that screaming?" people were saying.

"What's happened?"

"Is someone hurt?"

"What the hell is going on?"

"Oh my God, someone's been burnt!"

Bill, the owner, had led one of the waitresses out from the kitchen. She must have been the one who'd screamed in the dark. She was still sobbing and it was obvious why—all the way up her right side she was covered in burns. Her hand, arm, shoulder, and the right side of her face were completely covered in a mess of red and black bleeding flesh, so charred that it was hard to believe it had once been normal skin. Her hair was still smoking and the smell made me want to gag.

I heard someone on their phone calling an ambulance as other people moved forward, asking what had happened.

"I don't know," Bill said. He'd gone completely white. "I don't know how it happened. When the lights went out, she must have tripped or something. I think . . . I think she must have fallen against the deep-fat fryer . . ."

I could feel the blood pounding in my ears and turned back around to Jay. Wordlessly, he held up his phone for me to see. From the top of the screen to the bottom there was a huge crack running all the way down the glass.

"Did you . . . Did you drop it?" I asked.

But Jay just shook his head.

The ambulance arrived soon after that and took the weeping girl away.

"In all the years this place has been open we've never had an accident like this," I heard Bill say. "Never."

Bill went to the hospital with the girl, and the café closed early. Everyone filed away, going out to their cars and driving off. Soon Jay and I were the only ones left. Normally, he would have biked home and I would have waited by myself for my mom to pick me up, but today Jay said he would wait with me, and I was grateful to him for that.

"Thanks," I said. "And thanks for holding my hand when the lights went out."

He gave me a sharp look. "I didn't hold your hand."

A prickly feeling started to creep over my skin. "Yes, you did."

"Sophie, I didn't. You must have . . . You must have imagined it. It was pretty crazy in there."

I thought of those cold fingers curling around mine and shook my head. "Someone was definitely holding my hand when it went dark," I said. "And if it wasn't you, then who was it?"

"Well, it wasn't me. Maybe you've got a secret admirer."

"Did you see that girl standing on the table? I thought I saw her outline there in the dark."

Jay stared at me. "Are you actually trying to scare me right now? Because it's not going to work, you know. I'm not that gullible."

I glanced back through the windows of the café. There'd been no time to tidy up before the ambulance arrived and the place had been shut up as it was, with tables and chairs and broken china everywhere. A couple of the tables looked fairly normal, with plates of untouched food still on them, which was almost weirder.

I shivered and turned away, not wanting to look too closely in case I saw the girl among the empty tables.

"Look," Jay said. "It all got a bit crazy when the lights went out because of the waitress who hurt herself and started screaming. If it hadn't been for that, none of this would be any big deal. It was just a freak accident, that's all."

My mom pulled into the parking lot then, waving at me through the window.

"We could give you a lift," I said.

Jay's house wasn't very far away and he always biked home, but I couldn't stop thinking of that final question he had asked the Ouija board: *When will I die?*

"No thanks," Jay said. "I'll bike back."

I hesitated. "Jay . . ."

"You're not still worrying about that app, are you? Nothing's going to happen to me," he said. Then he grinned. "But just promise me one thing. If I *do* come to some appalling, grisly end tonight, I hope I can rely on you to tell the world it was a ghost that did me in."

For once I didn't smile. "Don't," I said. "Don't joke about it."

Jay laughed and put his arm around my shoulders in a friendly squeeze. "I think you really would miss me," he said.

Behind us, Mom honked her car horn to tell me to hurry up. Jay gave her a wave and said, "I'll see you tomorrow at school."

"All right. See you tomorrow."

I turned and started to walk across the parking lot but had only gone a few steps when I stopped and turned back. "Hey, Jay?"

"Yeah?"

"Will you do me a favor?"

"What is it?"

"Would you take the towpath tonight? Please?" Jay usually biked back home using the shortest route, which meant several busy roads. He did it all the time and nothing had ever happened to him. I knew I was being silly.

But if he went the other way, he'd miss all the major traffic and only add five minutes to his journey.

I was afraid that he'd refuse, or make a joke of it, or tease me again. But instead he just nodded.

"All right, Sophie. I'll take the towpath." Then he grinned, blew me a mock kiss, and said, "Anything for you."

I got into the front seat of Mom's car and waved at Jay as we drove past, keeping my eyes on him until the car turned the corner and I lost him from sight.

I didn't really want to talk to Mom about what had happened at the café, so when we got home I went straight upstairs and had a bath. Before going to bed I sent Jay a text to say good-night. It wasn't something I'd normally do, but I just wanted to reassure myself that he'd gotten home okay. He sent me a one-word answer: *Good-bye.*

I guessed he'd meant to say good-night but his auto-correct had changed it and he hadn't noticed. He'd replied, though, so at least I knew he was home. I got into bed and went to sleep.

I didn't remember until the next day that when Jay had shown me his phone at the café, it had been broken.

My dreams were filled with Ouija boards and burning hair and little girls holding my hand in the dark. And Jay inside a coffin. I tossed and turned all night. It was so bad that it was a relief to wake up, and I got out of bed in the morning without Mom having to drag me for a change.

With the sun shining in through the windows, the events of the night before started to seem less terrible. So the lights had gone out and someone had hurt themselves. It was horrible for that poor waitress but it had just been an accident, plain and simple. In the light of day, there didn't seem to be anything that strange about it.

I dressed quickly, for once actually looking forward to school. Jay would be outside soon and we'd walk there together, like we always did.

As I got ready I was vaguely aware of the phone ringing downstairs and the sound of Mom's voice as she answered it, but I didn't really pay it too much attention. By the time I went downstairs for breakfast, Mom was just hanging up.

"Who was that?" I asked.

She didn't answer straight away, and when I looked at her and saw her face I knew instantly that something was very wrong.

"What is it?" I said. "Who was that on the phone?"

"Sophie," Mom said, her voice all strained and weird-sounding. "I don't . . . I don't know how to tell you this . . . Sweetheart, you need to brace yourself—"

"Mom, *what*? What's wrong?"

"It's Jay. That was his dad on the phone. Something's happened. He . . . He never made it home last night."

"Yes, he did," I said at once. "He texted me."

But at that very second I remembered that Jay's phone was broken. I pulled my cell phone out of my pocket and started scrolling through, looking for his text, but it wasn't there.

"I don't understand. He sent me a text last night. I saw it."

"Sophie, he didn't send you a text. Oh, sweetheart, I'm so, so sorry, but . . . On the way home he had an accident. They think . . . They think that perhaps the brakes on his bike failed. He went into the canal. By the time they pulled him out, it was too late."

"What do you mean *too late*?" I said, clenching my hands so tight that I felt my nails tear the skin of my palms. "Jay's a strong swimmer. He won almost all the swim meets at school last year. If he'd fallen into the canal, he would have just swum to the side and climbed out."

But Mom was shaking her head. "They think he must have hit his head when he fell in. Sophie, he drowned."

It could not possibly be true. And yet, it was.

Jay was gone.

TWO

And yet on many a wintry night,
Young swains were gathered there.
For her father kept a social board,
And she was very fair.

I spent the next few days curled up in a ball under the covers of my bed, trying not to move, or breathe, or think, or fall asleep and dream about what had happened.

They think that perhaps the brakes on his bike failed . . .

I knew that Jay's old bike had been falling apart. That was why he'd been saving up for a new one. I tried to remember whether he'd said anything specifically about the brakes not working, but everything was a jumbled-up mess inside my head and I couldn't think straight. I just kept coming back to Jay standing there with his bike in the parking lot . . .

All right, Sophie. I'll take the towpath . . .

I didn't sleep that first night. I couldn't stop thinking about the Ouija board, or the girl I thought I'd seen in the café, or the cold fingers that had curled into my hand when it all went dark. Or Jay, lying on some undertaker's slab somewhere, all by himself.

The next day, in a kind of daze, I started reading about Ouija boards online, going through pages and pages of sites, squinting at the screen with raw and bloodshot eyes, and the more I read, the worse I felt. When I looked up the app itself, it was only to find that it had been taken down. There was a one-sentence explanation from the manufacturers stating that the app had been withdrawn due to complaints received from customers.

There were so many warnings about Ouija boards— people had been hurt using them, and others had died. One girl had posted a message on a forum saying: *Never, ever, ever use one of these things. They're not safe, and they're definitely not fun, and I just want to warn everyone so that no one else loses their best friend like I did.*

I shivered, wishing I had read her warning before Jay had downloaded that stupid app.

One of the sites said that if the planchette did a figure eight, it meant that an evil spirit was in control of the board. I thought back and tried to remember whether it had done that or not; it was hard to remember properly.

But there were two things I found out that disturbed me more than the rest. The first was the discovery that there were three questions you must never ask a Ouija board:

1. Never ask about God.
2. Never ask where the gold is buried.
3. Never ask when you're going to die.

And the second discovery—the one that made me feel worst of all—was a warning printed in bold text that said you must never, *ever* allow a planchette to count down through the numbers because a spirit could get out of the board that way.

But our planchette *had* counted down through the numbers. When it had gotten to zero, that was when the waitress in the kitchen had started screaming . . .

I tried to tell myself it was just a coincidence, that what had happened to Jay had nothing to do with Ouija boards or spirits or anything like that, but it didn't help because even if Jay's death *had* been an accident caused by his failing brakes, it was still my fault. I'd asked him to take the towpath. I had asked him to do that.

Anything for you . . .

The week passed in a blur of misery. I didn't know what to do with myself. Whenever I'd been unhappy before, it had always been Jay who would cheer me up. I kept expecting him to text me again, or walk through the door.

And whenever I was upstairs by myself I couldn't shake the sensation that there was someone there in the room with me, someone I couldn't see.

It was like there were hidden eyes staring and staring at me until my skin itched and my neck burned. I tried going downstairs, hoping that the feeling might go away if Mom was nearby, but it didn't make any difference.

One day I was sitting in front of the TV, still wearing my pajamas because getting dressed seemed like too much effort, when I could've sworn I felt icy-cold fingers brush against my face. I leaped to my feet, spilling the bowl of popcorn Mom had just brought me.

"Rebecca?" I said, staring around the room. "Are you there?"

But the room was empty.

Mom came in a moment later to see what all the fuss was about. "What's going on in here?" she asked.

"Mom." I swallowed hard and tried to sound normal. "Did you ever mess around with a Ouija board when you were younger?"

"What a strange question," Mom replied, bending down to gather up the popcorn. "Not that I can remember. Why?"

"It's just that . . . Jay and I were playing with one the night that . . . the night that he died."

"But where did you find one?" Mom asked, looking up at me.

"It wasn't an actual board—it was an app Jay had downloaded on his phone."

"Oh, one of those phone game things?"

"It wasn't a game, Mom, it . . . It said that Jay was going to die that night."

Mom stood up and came towards me. "Oh, Sophie, you're not going to let that upset you, are you? An app can't tell you when you're going to die."

"But it wasn't just an app, Mom, it was a Ouija board. I've read that they're supposed to be dangerous, that sometimes an evil spirit can—"

"Darling, what happened to Jay has got nothing to do with anything either one of you did that night." She hesitated a moment, then said, "Listen, why don't I call the school and see if you could go and talk with the counselor there? It might make you feel better to speak to a professional about it."

I was shaking my head before she'd even finished the sentence. "That's the last thing I want to do."

"All right," Mom said, holding up her hands and backing off. "It was just a suggestion."

I knew that nothing I said was going to convince her,

and yet my cheek still felt cold, as if icy fingers really had stroked my skin. I'd felt weirdly different ever since that night, but the feeling wasn't something I could explain, to Mom or to anyone.

I tried to tell myself it was just grief and guilt making me think strange things. After all, even if we had made contact with Rebecca, and even if she had escaped from the board, why would she have hurt Jay? He'd never done anything to her; he'd never even met her. But when I started to read about ghosts online I kept coming across the theory that if someone died under suspicious circumstances then they would become a vengeful spirit who wouldn't care who they hurt, and would just go on hurting people until they got justice. And I still didn't know how Rebecca had died.

I tried asking Mom later that day, but she just muttered something about an accident, and wouldn't say any more.

Promise me one thing, Jay had said. If anything happens to me, you'll tell the world it was a ghost . . . you'll tell the world . . .

Of course, he'd been joking, he hadn't meant any of it, and yet . . . somehow, the crazy thought lodged itself in my brain that I owed it to Jay to at least find out whether a spirit had had anything to do with his death. And if

Rebecca *had* been involved, well . . . I couldn't let her get away with it. I had to do *something*.

So when Dad came and told me that he and Mom were going to cancel their anniversary trip and stay at home with me instead, I said I didn't want them to, I still wanted to go and visit my uncle and cousins in Skye. Mom and Dad had been saving like mad for their trip to San Francisco and I knew they would lose the money if they canceled their flights. I told them everything they wanted to hear. "Being here will just remind me of what happened," I said. "I'll feel better somewhere else."

That wasn't true—all I wanted to do was cry in my room—but I must have been a better actress than I'd thought because, a week later, I was standing in the airport with my suitcase, waving good-bye to Mom and Dad.

First there was the flight to Glasgow, then I had to catch a train to Mallaig and then, finally, get the ferry to Skye. It was an insane place to get to, which was why I'd only met my cousins, Cameron, Piper, and Rebecca, once, when they came to stay seven years ago. Cameron was some kind of musical prodigy, and they'd come down especially so that he could play the piano for an important music teacher in London. And I'd never even met my cousin Lilias—Aunt Laura had been pregnant with her when I'd last seen the family.

I felt a bit nervous about seeing Cameron, Piper, and Lilias. It was too late to turn back now, though.

It had taken all day to get to Skye, and it was raining by the time I caught the ferry at Mallaig. It had been stiflingly hot the last couple of weeks so the rain was almost a relief, a fine summer drizzle that misted the air and clung to the ferry windows in big fat droplets, making it hard to see the island. I got my camera out of my bag, thinking that I might snap a photo as we approached, but really I think I just wanted to hold it and feel its familiar weight in my hands. It was my most prized possession.

The island emerged all of a sudden, huddled there in the water, starkly defined against the gray sky by jagged mountains that looked like they'd slice your hands open if you tried to climb them. What was I thinking, coming here like this? I could imagine what Jay would say.

"What's this?" he'd gasp in an exaggerated tone of mock surprise. "Ghost hunting? You know you won't last five minutes, right?"

It was probably true. I must have been insane to come here. What did I think I was going to be able to do? Track down Rebecca's vengeful spirit and somehow banish it to the other side?

"You ought to be flattered," I said to Jay inside my head. "You die and I go crazy. What a compliment."

I didn't know whether it was thinking about Jay, or

the choppiness of the sea, but I suddenly felt queasy, and I was glad when we pulled into the harbor at 6 p.m. It was pouring outside and the ferry speakers crackled to life as one of the staff made an announcement in a broad Scottish accent.

"Ladies and gentlemen, as you can see, Skye is living up to its Gaelic name today, *the Island of Mist,* so please mind your step on the gangplank, as it can get quite slippery out there. Welcome to the Sleat Peninsula, everyone, and enjoy your time on the island."

The gangplank led onto a sloped metal walkway that rose up out of the sea on stilts. The moment I stepped onto it, the wind whipped my hair around my face, and I could taste salt on my lips. By the time I reached the parking lot I was thoroughly soaked.

I stared around, wondering where Uncle James would be. I couldn't see him anywhere and, for a horrible moment, I was afraid he hadn't come. Maybe he'd forgotten or gotten the times mixed up. I felt a twist of panic and dumped my suitcase on the wet tarmac so I could take my phone from my pocket.

The hand that clapped down on my shoulder from behind made me jump and I whirled around to see my uncle standing there with an umbrella. Tall and dark-haired, he looked nothing like Mom, but then they were stepsiblings rather than blood ones.

"Sorry," he said. "I didn't mean to startle you. I wasn't sure it was you to begin with. You've grown up since I saw you last."

"It's . . . It's been a long time," I said, not sure what else to say.

"Yes, it has," Uncle James replied. "A long time. A very long time." He was looking at me, but his expression was distant and I wondered if he was remembering the last time we'd met, when Rebecca had still been alive. Then he shook his head and seemed to see me again. "You're soaked," he said. "Let's get you into the car."

I climbed into the front seat and shivered, wishing we were already at the house so that I could change into some dry clothes.

"I hope you had a good journey, anyway?" Uncle James said as he got in. "It's a long way to come on your own and this weather doesn't help. We don't have the best summers in Skye, I'm afraid."

"Is it always this foggy?" I asked. The fog seemed to be coming in off the sea in waves.

"Pretty much. The west coast is littered with ship-wrecks because of captains who thought the fog was thin and that they'd be able to see the island in time. Entire crews have drowned as a result."

The mention of drowning made me think of Jay again, but not the way I wanted to think of him, not the living, breathing, laughing best friend I'd always known, but a body sprawled by the side of the canal, soaking wet and stone cold and gone forever.

I felt suddenly tired. It was an hour and a half drive to the house and I leaned my head against the window, meaning to close my eyes for just a second, but I fell asleep right away and woke up some time later to Uncle James tapping my shoulder. The rain clouds and the fog made it seem very dark outside.

"We're here, Sophie," he said.

I rubbed the sleep from my eyes and looked up, expecting to see a house. But instead I saw gates looming before us in the harsh glare of the headlights. They were huge—two meters at least, set in a brick wall that was just as tall. A heavy-looking chain bound them together, and I watched as Uncle James got out and unlocked them before getting back into the car.

"I'll give you the code for the combination lock, but you must never leave the gates open," he said.

Daddy says never ever open the gate . . .

I sat up in my seat, suddenly wide awake. I was sure the Ouija-board app had said something just like that.

"Why?" My voice came out as a dry croak.

I saw Uncle James's mouth tighten. "It's not safe," he said. "In the morning you'll see—the house is on a clifftop. It's not safe in bad weather. Or after dark."

We drove through and he got out and locked the gate behind us. A long stone building huddled in the gleam of the headlights. I thought I saw a twitch of movement from one of the upstairs windows, as if a curtain had been pulled back and then quickly dropped. A strange little turret rose up from the center of the slate roof in the middle.

"What's that?" I asked, pointing at it.

"The old bell tower," Uncle James replied. "This used to be the schoolhouse. There's no bell there anymore, though. It's too windy here for that. It rang all the time and I couldn't concentrate on my paintings. Well, your cousins will certainly be keen to see you—Piper has talked of nothing else for days."

Now that I had finally arrived, I almost wished I was back on the ferry. I ran my fingers through my hair, hoping that it hadn't dried in too much of a mess. Uncle James parked the car and we got out, our feet crunching on the gravel drive. The sea breeze was cool against my skin and I could hear the distant crashing of waves somewhere out in the fog.

"What's that burning smell?" I asked, suddenly becoming aware of it—a smell of smoke and hot ash.

"I can't smell anything," Uncle James said and, weirdly, neither could I. The smell had disappeared all of a sudden, snatched away on the salty sea wind.

Uncle James took my suitcase from the trunk and I followed him into the house. We walked into a deserted entrance hall with a tiled floor and a steep staircase leading up to the first floor. I didn't like the look of that staircase. Something about it made my neck prickle. It was too tall and too steep. An accident waiting to happen. A staircase to break your neck on. And it was too warm inside the house, a stifling sort of airlessness that made sweat trickle down my back.

"That's funny," Uncle James said. "I thought they'd all be here to greet us."

At that moment a door opened to the left and a girl came out. She was my own age so I knew this must be Piper. I remembered her being pretty, but the girl who rushed forward to greet me wasn't just pretty, she was incredibly beautiful. She wore jeans and a simple pink sleeveless top with a high neckline. Her gorgeous strawberry blonde hair was pulled up into a thick ponytail and her eyes were a deep, sea-green color that made me think of mermaids.

I felt plain in comparison, and a little awkward, but Piper came right up and threw her arms around me as if we were long-lost sisters.

"Hello, Sophie," she said, hugging me tightly. "I'm so pleased that you've come to stay with us!"

"I'm glad too," I said, wishing I didn't sound so stiff and formal, and that my hair wasn't such a total mess.

"Where's Cameron?" Uncle James asked.

I saw Piper hesitate for a moment, as if she knew her dad wouldn't like the answer. Then she said, "I . . . I'm not sure. He might have gone to his room. I'm sure he wanted to be here to greet Sophie but I think maybe he wasn't feeling very well . . ."

"Don't try to cover up for him, Piper!" Uncle James said sharply. "He seemed perfectly fine when I left and I made it quite clear that he was to be here to greet his cousin when we arrived."

I felt awkward about Cameron getting into trouble on my account and thought I ought to say something. "That's all right—" I began.

"It's not all right," Uncle James cut me off. "It's extremely rude and I can only apologize on his behalf. I'm afraid you won't find Cameron quite as you remember him. He hasn't been the same since . . . well . . . Our family has had its share of troubles, as I'm sure you know."

I nodded and bit my tongue. I had to pick the right time to start asking questions about Rebecca and the second I arrived didn't seem quite appropriate.

"And what about Lilias?" Uncle James asked. "Has she suddenly fallen ill too?"

"She's up there, Dad," Piper said. "On the staircase."

34

I realized with a start that Piper was right—there *was* a girl sitting on the stairs, but she had been so silent and unmoving that I hadn't noticed her. Now I looked at the dark-haired girl staring down at us, unsmiling, from between the balustrades.

"Lilias, come down here and say hello to Sophie, please," Uncle James said.

Lilias got to her feet, but rather than coming down, she turned around and, without a word, ran back up the stairs. A second later, we heard a door slam.

"You mustn't mind Lilias," Uncle James said. "She's a nervous sort of child, but she'll soon get used to you. Piper, why don't you show Sophie around the house before dinner?"

"Of course. Come on, I'll give you the tour. We'll start with your room and you can dump your bag."

I picked up my suitcase and followed her up the stairs.

"These all used to be bedrooms for the schoolmistress and the girls back when this was a school," Piper said cheerfully. "This will be your room." She threw open the door closest to the stairs and we walked into a bedroom with big bay windows and a vase of purple butterwort flowers on the bedside table.

"I'm so pleased you're here," Piper said. "I could really use the company. Lilias is too young and Cameron . . .

well . . . he's not much fun these days, I'm afraid. Let's see if he's skulking in his room."

I felt a bit nervous as I followed her down the hall, but when Piper opened the door to Cameron's room, it was empty.

"I suppose he's gone off somewhere." Piper sighed. "You mustn't pay any attention to him, Sophie, the only thing he cares about is his music." I could tell as much from his bedroom, which was covered in loose piles of sheet music. "He really is very good, in spite of his . . . well, his injury. He'll never be quite as accomplished as he was before, though, so you have to make allowances for him. I think that's why he can be a bit . . . just a bit abrupt sometimes. He doesn't mean it. That's what I try to remember when he says cruel things to me, and you must do the same."

I thought back to meeting Cameron when we were kids and remembered him as a fun, good-natured boy who'd made a real effort to include me in games with his sisters. I found it hard to imagine him saying cruel things to anyone.

"He won't be like you remember him," Piper said, as if reading my mind.

"What did you mean about him having an injury?" I asked. "I don't remember that."

"Oh, it was after we came to see you," Piper replied.

"He hurt his hand. In the fire. But don't mention it to him, whatever you do—he's terribly sensitive about it."

She showed me the other upstairs rooms—except for the one in between my room and Lilias's.

"What's in there?" I asked, pointing at the closed door.

"We . . . We don't use that room," Piper said. "Not anymore." She glanced at me and added under her breath, "It used to be my sister's room, you see. Rebecca's."

"Oh."

Her cheerful tone had disappeared for the first time since I'd arrived, so I didn't dare ask anymore questions. We went downstairs and Piper showed me the rest of the house, the heart of which was a huge, long room with a lofty vaulted ceiling, full-length windows and an actual stage at one end.

"This used to be the school hall," Piper said. "That's why it's so big. The pupils used to come here for assembly, and they performed their school plays on that stage there."

It was both a dining and sitting room, with a dining table at one end and a couch area at the other. I felt a bit unnerved by the tall windows running down its length. It still wasn't dark outside but the rain clouds cloaked everything in shadow, and the effect of so many uncovered windows made it seem like the gloom was pressing in against the glass, trying to get into the house. I was used to curtains at home, and these bare windows made me feel like anyone could be staring in at us from outside and we would have no idea.

A massive black piano gleamed in the center of the stage. Piper scrambled up onto it and I followed her.

"This is Cameron's piano," she said, running her hand over the smooth, polished surface. "It's a baby grand. Dad bought it for him before his accident, back when we all thought he was going to be the next Mozart or something. It's worth an absolute fortune—Dad had to remortgage the house to buy it. It's Cameron's pride and joy. Sometimes I think he cares about this piano more than he cares about any of us." She laughed, but it came out kind of hollow.

Next, we went into a room that smelled of chalk, with a big blackboard attached to one wall and three old-fashioned desks lined up in front of it. "This was one of the classrooms," Piper said. "Those desks are from the original school. Cameron, Rebecca, and I used to do our homework here, and Lilias still does during exam time. Look, this photo is of the school in 1910."

She pointed at the framed black-and-white photo hanging on the wall. It showed the house, looking exactly the same except that it didn't have the high wall built around it, and you could clearly see the bell in the bell tower. A class of children were lined up outside the front door—there were about twenty of them, all girls, aged seven or eight. A teacher stood next to them, unsmiling, with her hands clasped primly in front of her. She looked plain and extremely serious. The children looked very serious too.

"I don't think they had much fun in the olden days, do you?" Piper asked with a laugh.

There was one girl in particular who caught my eye. She was in the front row, beside the teacher, and she was facing the photographer but she wouldn't have been able to see him because she had a piece of cloth tied over her eyes. It reminded me of the blindfolds they covered someone's eyes with when they were about to be executed.

"Why is that girl wearing a blindfold?" I asked, pointing at her.

Piper shrugged. "I don't know. She must have had something wrong with her eyes, I suppose. Maybe she was blind?"

There were other photos on the wall, family photos. And one of them showed Cameron, Piper, and Rebecca. It must have been taken around the time they came to visit because they looked just as I remembered them. Cameron stood between his sisters, with an arm around each of them—he was smiling into the camera and so were the two girls. My eyes were drawn instantly to Rebecca. She had been incredibly pretty, with long black hair and violet eyes.

"That was one of the last photos taken of Rebecca," Piper said at my side. She sighed and said, "We look so happy, don't we? I often look at this photo and wish I could go back to that moment. That I could warn them all about what was going to happen to us."

As she spoke she glanced at a photo of Aunt Laura that was hanging on the wall. Piper had clearly inherited her looks from her mom—they were very much alike, right down to the strawberry blonde hair. "Do you ever see her?" I asked.

I didn't know much about Aunt Laura, only that she'd had a nervous breakdown a couple of years ago and been committed to some kind of hospital.

Piper shook her head. "Dad visits her sometimes, but the doctors don't think it will help her recovery to see us kids right now, so we don't go. She just couldn't cope after Rebecca died. Sometimes I wonder if that's why Lilias is always so serious, you know? Mom cried every single day in the months before she was born. Cameron makes Lilias smile sometimes, but he's the only one who can. And she never laughs."

"Never?"

"Not that I've seen. I don't think she knows how, poor thing. Anyway, I'd better go and finish dinner. You've got time to go and freshen up if you want to."

I went back upstairs to my bedroom, where I changed into some fresh clothes and brushed my hair. When I opened the door to go back downstairs, Lilias was standing in the corridor. She was wearing jeans and a long-sleeved turtleneck, which surprised me—it was so muggy and warm inside the house, I'd swapped my top for a T-shirt. In her hands she held a soft toy ostrich.

"Hello," I said. Then I gestured to her ostrich and added, "What's your friend's name?"

I half thought she might run away again, but instead she held up her toy for me to see and said, "This is my ostrich. Her name is Hannah. She's my best friend. She never says bad things to me. She never tells me to do horrible things."

"Er . . . that's good," I said.

"Who's your friend?" Lilias asked.

"What friend?"

"The girl that came here with you."

I stared at her. "No one came with me."

"Yes, she did," Lilias insisted. She pointed at Rebecca's closed door and added, "She just went in there. She said it was her room but that's not true. That's my sister's room."

I stared at her again. "No one came here with me, Lilias."

"She was holding your hand when you walked through the front door."

I swallowed hard and, in my best, firm, grown-up voice, said, "That's not true."

She scowled at me. "It *is* true," she said. "I don't tell lies. *You're* the liar. I think you knew she was holding your hand all along. I think you brought her to our house on purpose. I wish you hadn't come! I don't like you and neither does Hannah!"

And with that she ran straight past me, down the stairs and out of sight. So far I was doing a pretty pathetic job of trying to make friends with her. I stared after her for a second and then, slowly, turned my eyes to Rebecca's closed door. I walked over and paused outside it. Then I reached out and brushed my fingertips lightly against its surface.

The next second I gasped and snatched my hand back. The door was icy cold to the touch, but it wasn't just the coldness that shocked me—it was the sudden sense of stone-cold evil I could feel radiating from the shut-up room. I couldn't have put the feeling into words, not in a way that would make sense to anyone else, but it was dark and horrible and malevolent, and it made me feel slightly sick.

I shivered and rubbed at the goosebumps on my arms. I felt a sudden urge to run—run as far away from this place as I could and never, ever look back. But, as I stood there staring at the door, I heard a thump, as if something heavy had just fallen to the floor.

And I could have sworn the sound came from inside Rebecca's room.

THREE

One New Year's Eve as the sun went down,
Far looked her wishful eye.
Out from the frosty window pane,
As merry sleighs went by.

I stared at the door in front of me, hesitated for a moment, and then stepped closer, my whole body tense. A moment of silence passed, so I put my ear to the door, listening as hard as I could—

"Can I help you with something?"

I hadn't heard anyone come up behind me, so I almost jumped out of my skin at the sound of the voice. When I turned around I saw a tall boy standing there. He was dark-haired, unsmiling, and, strangely, dripping wet. His jeans were sodden and his dark T-shirt was clinging to him beneath his jacket. I knew this must be Cameron because he was the only teenage boy in the house, but I would never have recognized him from before.

He was a year older than me at sixteen, and he had the pale, serious look of someone who never smiled or laughed. But there was something oddly handsome about him, and I was so aware of his cheekbones and the shape of his chest through his wet T-shirt that I began to feel quite embarrassed. His blue eyes were staring at me so intensely that it was like he could read my mind and already knew every secret thought I'd ever had.

"Oh!" I said. "No. Sorry. I was just . . . I thought I heard a noise in there."

"You couldn't have," Cameron replied in a cold voice. "No one uses that room anymore."

I swallowed. "Right. I'm . . . I'm Sophie, by the way."

"I know who you are," he said. "Why are you here?"

His question startled me. I wasn't entirely sure whether he meant here outside Rebecca's room or here in the house. "Just . . . Just for a visit. Why are you soaking wet?"

"I went for a walk," he replied shortly. Then he added, unnecessarily, "It's raining again."

He stalked past me and disappeared into his bedroom. I stared after him, wondering what I'd said that had annoyed him so much.

I went downstairs and met Piper in the entrance hall.

"I was just coming to call you for dinner," she said. "Did you pass Cameron on the way down?"

"Yes," I replied, not really knowing what to say about the awkward exchange.

"I suppose you noticed he's soaking wet?" Piper said. "Please don't tell Dad that he's been outside. None of us are supposed to leave the house if the weather's bad. Dad will go mad if he finds out."

"Of course," I replied. The last thing I wanted was to get Cameron in trouble, especially since he already seemed to have taken a disliking to me.

Piper smiled and then called up the stairs, "Cameron! Dinner's ready!"

He didn't reply, but she didn't seem to expect him to.

"Come on," she said. "Dad and Lilias are already in there."

I followed her to the hall. The lights on the sitting-room side were switched off but the spotlights above the dining table were turned on, bathing the table in a pool of too-bright light that threw everything else into shadow. Uncle James and Lilias were already sitting there and, for a weird moment, the spotlights on them almost made it look like this was the stage of a play and they were just actors in it, rather than a family about to eat dinner.

I followed Piper across the room to the table. Uncle James sat at one end with Lilias to his right. "I set your place here next to me," Piper said. "Sit down and I'll get the food."

She left the room and came back a moment later with a large dish of vegetables, which she placed in the middle of the table. Cameron arrived just as she headed back into the kitchen.

"Oh, so you've decided to grace us with your presence at last?" Uncle James said as Cameron pulled out the chair at the opposite end of the table. I noticed that he kept his right hand hidden in his pocket and only used his left. He'd towel-dried his hair but it was still noticeably damp and I wondered if Uncle James suspected that he'd been outside. "Have you said hello to your cousin at least?"

"We met upstairs," Cameron replied, without looking at me.

"Here we are," Piper said brightly, appearing with two steaming plates in her hands. "Eat up before it gets cold."

It was steak with a béarnaise sauce on top. I was very impressed—I could barely manage to produce beans on toast or boil an egg, but when I said as much, Piper laughed. "I probably shouldn't admit this but I didn't cook it myself. It's one of those luxury ready meals. I wanted to serve something a bit more exciting than pizza for your first night with us."

"It looks wonderful," Uncle James said.

"Yes, this looks very appetizing, Piper, but how exactly am I supposed to eat it?" Cameron asked from the end of the table.

"Oh." Piper looked flustered. "Oh, I'm sorry, I didn't think. Here, let me cut it up for you."

I watched in surprise as Piper got to her feet, rushed to Cameron's side, and proceeded to cut his steak up into bite-size chunks, while he held his fork loosely in his left hand and watched her with an unreadable expression on his face. It was an embarrassing moment and no one offered any explanation, but I realized that Cameron's burnt hand must mean that he couldn't use a knife properly.

"Your mother tells me you're quite the photographer, Sophie," Uncle James said.

"Oh, well . . . I'm nothing special or anything but I do enjoy taking photos," I said. I was very aware of Cameron's blue eyes fixed on me from the other end of the table.

"It's no use trying to keep young people inside, I know," Uncle James said, "but I must insist that you stick to the paths. There are some beautiful clifftop walks around here but it isn't safe to wander from them. Just this summer a tourist died when he went too close to the edge." He shook his head. "Such a waste. Apparently he was trying to get a better photograph to take home with him, but I hope I can trust you to be more sensible than that? And make sure you go with Piper or Cameron the first time. They know which areas are safe and which aren't."

"We'll go and explore tomorrow," Piper said, smiling at me.

"And Lilias," Uncle James said, "don't you have something to say to your cousin?"

"Sorry for running away, and not giving you a proper welcome, and being so rude," Lilias said, like an actor reading out one of her lines.

"That's all right," I said, giving her a smile.

"I drew you a picture," Lilias said.

"Good girl," Uncle James said in an approving tone.

She produced a piece of paper from underneath the table and started to slide it across to me. I saw Cameron glance at the drawing as it went past his plate and then, inexplicably, he dropped his fork, snatched the drawing from Lilias, and crumpled it up in his fist.

"Cameron!" Uncle James snapped. "Don't start any of your nonsense. Give the drawing to Sophie."

"I don't think she wants this one," Cameron replied, quite calmly.

"Give it to her now," Uncle James said through gritted teeth.

For a moment they stared at each other across the table. Finally, Cameron shrugged and straightened out the drawing as best he could with only one hand. His right remained hidden from sight under the table. He handed the drawing to me with a look that was almost apologetic.

As soon as I took the drawing, I knew why he hadn't wanted me to see it. Lilias had drawn the picture using just two crayons, black and red. It was a house with a family lined up outside it—so far, so normal—except the family were all dead. There seemed to be parents and three children, and they were all lying in puddles of blood, scribbled in with angry, jagged red lines. At the top, in her childish, wobbly handwriting, Lilias had written a title for her ghoulish picture: *The Murder House.*

"He killed them all while they were asleep," Lilias said, in the same self-satisfied tone of voice in which a magician would say "ta-da!" after finishing a magic trick.

"Who did?" Uncle James said, giving her a startled look.

"No one knows. They never caught him."

"She's been watching that unsolved crime show again," Cameron said, picking up his fork and returning to his dinner as if this was something quite normal. "She drew another one of those murder scenes."

"Oh, Lilias," Uncle James groaned. "For heaven's sake, why couldn't you have drawn a flower or something?" He glanced at me and said, "I'm sorry—she's going through a bit of a macabre phase at the moment. I suppose all children do at some point, don't they?"

I nodded, but couldn't remember a time when I'd ever gone around drawing grisly murder scenes and presenting them to people as gifts.

"It happened at night," Lilias said, looking at me. "They all went to bed and someone killed them while they were asleep. He hacked them up with an axe as they lay in their beds. *Chop, chop!* Like that."

"Lilias, that's enough!" Uncle James said. He sounded exasperated. "Not at the dinner table, please. Remember your manners."

"Sophie will think she's come to a house of horrors," Piper said with a forced laugh. She turned to Cameron and said, "You must play the piano for Sophie while she's here." She spoke in a bright tone and I guessed she was trying to get the conversation back to a more normal topic. "Perhaps you could play something after dinner?"

She glanced to the other end of the room. With the lights turned off, the stage and the piano were cloaked in shadows, so when a discordant chord suddenly rang out, I almost jumped out of my seat, my knife and fork falling to the table with a clatter.

"Who's that?" I asked, straining my eyes in the direction of the stage, trying to make out the piano and wondering whether there could be a fifth member of the

Craig family I didn't know about. Someone was pressing the piano keys on the other side of the room. There came several more chords, all wrong and out of tune, as if the person didn't know how to play and was just pressing keys at random.

Cameron laughed, the first time I'd heard him do so since I'd arrived. But it wasn't a friendly sound. "Relax," he said. "It's only Shellycoat."

There was more tuneless clanging, a soft thump, and, a few seconds later, a gray cat trotted out of the shadows and jumped straight onto Cameron's lap. "I must have forgotten to close the lid over the keys," Cameron said, still looking amused.

I looked down at my food, feeling embarrassed. "Shellycoat is an unusual name for a cat," I said, just for the sake of saying something.

"Oh, she's named after a Scottish folk legend," Piper said. "A shellycoat is a kind of Scottish monster. It haunts streams and rivers and has long, wet black hair and wears a coat of shells—small ones from water snails and whelks and things like that, which means you can hear it coming at least. If they're not able to drown people, shellycoats delight in humiliating them instead, so they say."

This was the second time today someone had mentioned drowning to me. It wouldn't have bothered me before Jay died, but since then I didn't want to hear that word or think about it. I still wasn't sure whether Uncle James and his family knew what had just happened to my best friend, but Piper seemed to sense my discomfort because hurriedly she changed the subject by gesturing towards the cat and saying, "Rebecca named her."

At the mention of her name, there was a sudden total silence. Everyone seemed to freeze in their seats. Rebecca's death had been a tragedy, so I hadn't expected her to be a lighthearted subject, but I hadn't expected this kind of reaction either. Everyone was staring at Piper as if she'd just said the foulest swear word imaginable.

Cameron was the first to recover. He skewered a bite-size chunk of his steak and put it in his mouth, chewing it slowly, watching Piper the whole time. Uncle James set his glass down on the table so hard that some wine slopped out of it, staining the tablecloth. Lilias slammed her knife down into her steak, and there was a thud as it made contact with bone.

And that was when she started screaming.

It was a proper, bloodcurdling shriek that made the hair on the back of my neck stand up. For a confused moment I was sure Lilias must have chopped her finger off, the way she was yelling. If there had been any neighbors nearby, they would surely have called the police, convinced that a murder was being committed.

With a hiss, the cat shot out of Cameron's lap, and he

was on his feet a second later, closely followed by Uncle James. They both rushed over to Lilias, and Cameron shoved her plate of food across the table, as if it were a bomb that might go off at any second. I noticed that Cameron's hand was bleeding and realized that the cat must have scratched him as it ran away. A few drops fell onto the tablecloth.

"It's all right, Lilias," Cameron said. "Remember what you have to do. Just breathe. Just breathe."

I could see Lilias trying, but it was as if she was so terrified that she couldn't physically draw in the air. She was shaking from head to toe, like she was having some kind of fit. It took them several minutes to calm her down, all the while Piper kept saying, over and over again, "I'm sorry, I'm so sorry. The packet said they were boneless. I checked and *double*-checked!"

Finally, when Lilias had calmed down a little, Cameron said, "I'll take her to bed." And in one fluid motion he picked her up and she wrapped both arms around his neck, her face pressed into his shoulder. He scooped up the ostrich, lying discarded on the table, and strode from the room without another word.

Uncle James sat down heavily in his chair, Piper had both hands clamped over her mouth and, for a moment, there was a strained silence.

"Is . . . Is she going to be okay?" I finally asked.

"She'll be fine," Uncle James replied. "You must be wondering about what you just saw, Sophie. I'm afraid that Lilias has a condition. She's receiving treatment for it. She goes to a therapist in town once a week."

"What kind of condition?" I asked.

"It's called cartilogenophobia," Uncle James said. "Fear of bones."

Piper lowered her hands from her mouth and I could see that they were trembling slightly. "I don't know how this could have happened," she whispered. "The box said there were no bones. There must have been some mix-up at the factory. I'm so sorry, Dad."

"It's not your fault," Uncle James replied. He glanced at me and said, "You might as well know that Lilias is scared of all bones, even the ones inside her own body. She's been gradually improving since she started therapy, but we never serve any food with bones in it and . . . and just as an extra precaution we keep all the kitchen knives in a locked drawer. A couple of years ago Lilias got hold of one and tried to cut out one of her collarbones. She survived, obviously—Cameron caught her in the act, otherwise God knows what would have happened, and I don't think she'd try to do it again, but . . . we don't want to take any chances."

"Of course not," I said, hardly knowing what else to say. I wondered whether that was why Lilias had been wearing a turtleneck—to hide whatever scars remained from what she'd tried to do.

Cameron and Lilias did not return to the table and their food slowly congealed and cooled on their plates. Piper, Uncle James, and I finished our meals in strained silence, and it was a relief when it was over and I could finally return to my bedroom.

The smell of rotting flowers greeted me as soon as I opened the door. To my surprise, the purple butterworts on my bedside table seemed to have shriveled up and died while I'd been downstairs. The change seemed so fast that I almost wondered whether someone could have sneaked in here and swapped the living flowers for dead ones.

As I got changed I wondered what on earth Jay would say about all this if he were here. Probably something like: "They're all barking mad, Sophie. I'd bolt if I were you, before they turn you into a basket case too. I'll still come and visit you in the loony bin, though—if you go off your rocker, I mean. You'll always have me. You know that, right?"

Sometimes I could hear his voice so clearly in my mind that it was almost like he was still here with me, like I could reach out and touch him.

"I won't leave," I said, talking to Jay even though I knew he wasn't really there. "No matter how much I want to, I won't leave until I find out the truth about what happened to you."

The room felt muggy and warm, but when I went over to the window to let in a blast of fresh sea air, I found that it had been sealed shut with some kind of black sealing wax. The window wouldn't budge—I couldn't even open it a crack.

I groaned. It was so hot—perhaps those flowers had died naturally after all. I switched off the lamp, climbed into bed, and tried to lie as still as possible so that I might cool down a bit.

I didn't think I would fall asleep very easily that night, but in fact I fell asleep almost as soon as I lay down, and probably would have slept soundly all the way through till morning if I hadn't been woken up a few hours later by cold fingers wrapping themselves tightly around my ankle.

FOUR

In a village fifteen miles away,
Was to be a ball that night.
And though the air was heavy and cold,
Her heart was warm and light.

The fingers were cold as ice, so cold that they seemed to burn and blister my skin. I gasped in the dark and tried to sit up to reach for the bedside lamp, but then another cold hand grabbed my wrist and pinned it to the bed. Fingers combed through my hair, yanking my head back down to the pillow. And suddenly there were cold hands all over me—they seemed to come straight up out of the bed, pinching and scratching and clawing at my skin, like a hundred tiny birds pecking me to death.

I opened my mouth to scream and found the hands were in my mouth as well, tiny little cold fingers far too small to be human. They were more like dolls' hands, squeezing around my tongue, scratching at my teeth, poking the inside of my mouth, and crawling down my throat, choking me and making it impossible to breathe.

I thrashed and flailed and fought them as hard as I could, but I was helpless in the grip of so many hands and I knew that they were winning. I knew that they meant to kill me.

Then a voice whispered in my ear, and it was a warm, sweet voice, a voice I knew so well.

"Wake up, Sophie," Jay said. "It's only a dream. Time to wake up now."

And I could have cried because Jay wasn't really dead, he was right here with me and it had all just been a terrible nightmare. The knowledge gave me the strength to fight the cold hands that were trying to drag me down into the darkness. With a final burst of effort I managed to yank one of my arms free and lash out at them. My hand slapped someone hard in the dark. I felt skin tear and warm blood seep out beneath my nails.

And then that voice again: "Wake *up*, Sophie! You're dreaming!"

Only it wasn't Jay's voice this time; it was Cameron's.

I blinked in confusion, trying to work out what was happening. The lights were on and I saw that I was in the guest bedroom at Uncle James's house. Cameron was leaning over me, his dark hair all tousled from sleep, both hands gripping my arms. A deep scratch ran down his cheek, bleeding slightly.

"You're dreaming," he said again. "It's just a nightmare—you're safe."

Cameron's left hand felt warm and normal on my skin but his right felt strange—hard and rubbery, as if he was wearing some kind of glove. I looked down and gasped in shock at the sight of his right hand. Even though I'd known it was burnt, I wasn't prepared for the sight of that shriveled, ruined skin that completely covered his palm and reached all the way up past his wrist.

It reminded me of the waitress back at the café. I could still hear her scream ringing in my ears, could still smell that awful scent of burning hair and human flesh. I shuddered at the memory, but Cameron clearly thought it was the sight of his hand that had made me shudder. He snatched his hands away as if I'd given him an electric shock and stepped back from the bed so fast that he stumbled slightly. His trousers didn't have any pockets so he put his hand behind his back instead.

"I'm sorry," he said stiffly. "I wouldn't have come in here like this, only I heard you cry out and I thought—" He broke off abruptly, and I got the impression that he'd suddenly changed his mind about what he'd been going to say. "I thought you might wake the whole house," he said instead.

Despite the fact I knew it had just been a dream, I still felt the need to look around the bed, still half expecting to see hands poking up out of the mattress or curling around the pillow. Of course, there was nothing there but crumpled sheets, damp with sweat. The room was hot enough to suffocate.

"I'm sorry," I said. "It was just . . . I guess I was having a nightmare."

"So it would seem," he replied. He raised an eyebrow. "Is this going to happen every night, do you think?"

I could feel myself blushing furiously. Cameron hadn't exactly seemed delighted to see me as it was, and waking him up in the middle of the night like this was definitely not giving a good first impression. "It's never happened before," I said. Then I saw the scratch on his face and groaned aloud before I could stop myself. "Did I do that?"

"I couldn't wake you," he replied. Then added, "You're stronger than you look."

"I'm really sorry," I said again.

He inclined his head slightly. "Forget it. It's not the first time I've been slapped by a girl, and I'm sure it won't be the last. Do you think you'll be all right now?"

"Yes," I said, feeling embarrassed. "Sorry."

"You don't need to keep apologizing," Cameron said, already turning away.

I called good-night to him but he didn't reply as he walked out the door, carefully moving his burnt hand in front of him so that I wouldn't see it as he left.

I lay awake for the next few minutes feeling terrible, hating myself for reacting to Cameron's hand like that. If I hadn't still been half tangled up in the nightmare, as well as reminded of that burnt waitress, I would never have behaved that way.

When I lay back down on the pillows, I still felt afraid of the bed, half fearing that the cold hands might come back the moment I turned out the light.

I shook my head, disgusted with myself. I'd be screaming at shadows next. I reached out and firmly snapped off the light.

The moment I did so, someone downstairs started to laugh.

It wasn't like any laughter I had ever heard before and I turned the light back on at once.

Then the laugh came again.

God, it was a weird sound, and suddenly I was sitting bolt upright, my heart thumping in my chest. The laughter was shrill and high-pitched but it sounded all wrong, as if the person wasn't actually amused and didn't even understand what laughter was, but was just going through the motions of making the sound.

I made myself get out of bed and tiptoe out to the

banister. I knew it looked over the entrance hall by the front door but, in the darkness, I couldn't see whoever was down there. I could hear them, though, clearer than ever. And, as I stood there, the laughing stopped and the person suddenly spoke.

"*Monstrous,*" they said, quite clearly. Then, "*Monstrous, monstrous.*"

A cold horror prickled over my skin. There was something wrong with the voice, something dreadfully wrong, as if the speaker was not quite right in the head, demented somehow, or inhuman in some way. No normal person would speak like that. I couldn't even tell if it was male or female. It was high-pitched but didn't quite sound like either. Whoever they were, they were down there in the lobby, talking to themselves in the dark.

I thought of the awful murder scene that Lilias had been talking about at dinner, and I knew I had to wake someone up and tell them there was an intruder so that we could call the police. I wondered how long it would take for them to arrive at this lonely clifftop spot. The nearest house must be several miles away. We could all be butchered in our beds and no one would find out about it for hours and hours.

"*Never do that again,*" the high voice downstairs said. "*Never do that again. There's blood under the rug!*"

I backed away from the banister, trying to remember where Uncle James's room was but, at that moment, a door down the corridor opened and Cameron stepped out. Despite the heat, he'd put on a dressing gown over his pajamas, and his right hand was buried in his pocket.

I gestured to him frantically. "There's someone down there!" I whispered as he came towards me.

"Yes, I know," Cameron replied. "It's Dark Tom."

"Monstrous," the voice said softly. *"Monstrous."*

My fingers gripped the banister hard. "Who's Dark Tom?" I whispered.

"Piper's African gray, of course." Then, when I still looked blank, Cameron added, "Her pet parrot. His cage is tucked into the alcove by the front door. Didn't she introduce you to him?"

I was so relieved that I could have hugged him. "No, she didn't," I said, relaxing my grip on the banister.

"I suppose you imagined that we were all about to be axed in our beds by a lunatic," Cameron said. "I did try to warn you not to look at Lilias's drawing." In the dim light I couldn't see his face clearly, but I could hear the amusement in his voice. "Are you always this nervous?" he asked.

"He just startled me," I snapped. "That's all. How many words can he say, anyway?"

"Oh, loads. He's got an amazing vocabulary. We loved

teaching him new words when we were kids. He'll repeat anything if he hears it often enough. Sometimes he'll even repeat things he's heard only once."

"He was talking about blood under the rug."

"Yes. Well. Dark Tom's heard a lot of unspeakable things in this house, I'm afraid. Don't be offended if he starts swearing at you. His manners are appalling. He's a horrible old thing, really. I don't know why we put up with him." Cameron leaned over the banister and said in a harsh whisper, "Tom! Be quiet! Or you'll get no fruit for breakfast tomorrow!"

"Blood," Dark Tom said sullenly, *"under the rug."*

"I mean it, Tom!" Cameron hissed.

And the parrot finally fell silent.

"Well," Cameron said, turning to me and raising his eyebrow slightly, "what an exciting night we seem to be having. If Tom wakes you again just tell him to pipe down. You have to be firm with him. Get Piper to introduce you in the morning. But don't expect him to make friends with you; he pretty much hates everyone. And don't stick your fingers into his cage, whatever you do. He'll have them off if he gets half the chance."

"Thanks for the advice," I said. "And for . . . for earlier."

Cameron looked at me in the dark and there was silence between us for a moment. I heard him draw breath and thought he was going to say something else but, in the end, he just said, "Well, good-night then."

And he went back to his room, closing the door firmly behind him.

⸻

There were no more disturbances that night and I managed to sleep until the morning. When I woke up, the first thing I noticed was the dappled light dancing on the ceiling, reflecting off the sea, and the sound of seagulls calling to each other in the distance.

I got up and went to the window, which looked out on the garden at the back of the house, with the ocean beyond. But the thing that caught my attention straight away was the burnt tree. It was a black, dead thing, with spindly branches poking up into the air like twisted fingers. It was hard to tell because everything was so dark, but I thought I could make out a few rotting planks of wood nestled among the branches, as if there'd been some kind of tree house there once.

When I looked at my watch, I was startled to see that it was past ten. I'd slept much later than I'd meant to, so I dressed quickly in a tank top and jeans and went downstairs. Now that the sun was shining through the windows, I noticed the alcove Cameron had mentioned. The parrot's cage was tucked in the corner, almost out of sight. He was extremely handsome, with sleek gray feathers and keen, intelligent eyes that watched me the entire time.

"Hello," I said. "You gave me quite a fright last night."

"Fright," Dark Tom said, tilting his head this way and that, as if trying the new word out to see if he liked it. *"Fright. Fright. Fright!"*

Although I knew the parrot didn't understand the word, and that he was only repeating it back at me, he seemed to say it with a kind of relish that sent a shiver down my spine.

Piper must have heard me come down because she emerged from the living room a second later.

"You naughty thing, waking Sophie up like that!" Her strawberry blonde hair was down today, tumbling loose over her shoulders in soft waves that made her look even more like a mermaid.

She gave me an apologetic look and said, "Cameron told me Tom gave you a scare in the night. I'm so sorry."

"That's okay. It's lucky Cameron came out when he did or I might have woken your dad up over a parrot!"

"Oh, Cameron can't stand Tom talking in the night. He's a chronic insomniac. Cameron, that is, not Tom! It's because he broods over things so much, that's what I think. If he'd lighten up a bit and have some fun he'd probably sleep like a baby. Would you like some breakfast?

Afterwards, perhaps we can go for a walk along the clifftop?"

"Sounds good. How's Lilias?" I asked as we walked into the kitchen.

"Oh, she's all right. She's always better after a good night's rest. Sit down and I'll make some toast."

I pulled up a chair, and Shellycoat jumped straight onto my lap.

"She must like you," Piper said, surprised. "She doesn't normally take to strangers."

I ate my toast with one hand and stroked Shellycoat with the other. I could see she was quite an old cat. She only had a handful of teeth left and she was rather bony, but she purred the whole time I was stroking her.

"What's wrong with her eye?" I asked.

Now that I could see her more closely, I realized that one of her eyelids was closed tight.

"She's blind in that eye," Piper said.

"Oh, was she born like that?"

Piper hesitated a moment, then said, "No, she wasn't born like that. She used to be Rebecca's cat, you see."

I frowned and was about to ask what she meant, but Piper was already heading for the door.

"Shall we go now, if you're finished?" she said over her shoulder.

"Let me just grab my camera."

I went upstairs to fetch it and, a few minutes later, Piper was unlocking the heavy chain around the gate.

"Did Dad explain to you about the gate?" she asked.

"You mean that it must always stay locked?"

Piper nodded. "He's absolutely paranoid about something happening to Lilias."

"Is that why my bedroom window is sealed shut?"

"Oh, all the upstairs windows are, but it wasn't Dad who did that. Apparently there was some kind of accident back when the house used to be a school. One of the girls fell from an upstairs window."

"How awful! Was she okay?"

"No, she died. They sealed the windows after that."

We locked the gate carefully behind us and then set out along the path. It hugged the edge of the clifftop and I could see at once why it was dangerous. There were no barriers of any kind and it was a sheer drop to the rocks below. The wind hadn't died down much since yesterday, and seemed to tug at my sleeve like invisible hands trying to pull me over the edge. When I asked Piper about it, she said, "They did talk about putting fences up once but there's miles of open croft land and moorland around here and it would cost a fortune to put fences up everywhere. What do you think? It's beautiful, isn't it?"

It was certainly beautiful, but there was one part of the scene that made me feel cold all over—and that was the sand down on the beach. I had imagined it being a warm, golden color but, instead, it was completely black, like mud.

Black sand . . .

Suddenly I was back in the café, watching the Ouija-board app spell out those words.

Frozen Charlotte, black sand . . .

"Do you know anyone called Charlotte?" I asked Piper.

She looked surprised. "Charlotte? Not that I can think of. Why?"

"Never mind. It doesn't matter."

We walked along the path while Piper chattered away, pointing out birds and plants and rocks. But after five minutes I couldn't contain the question any longer.

"What did you mean about Shellycoat earlier?"

"Shellycoat?"

"Yes, you said she was Rebecca's cat, as if that explained why she's blind in one eye."

Piper came to a stop in the middle of the path. "Oh," she said. "I just assumed that you knew. I forgot you only met Rebecca once." She looked at me, strands of hair blowing around her face, and said, "If you'd known her a little better it would make sense to you. Rebecca was . . . well, she had a bit of a cruel streak, I'm afraid, and Shellycoat probably just got in her way one day. Or maybe she had nothing else to do."

I stared at her. "Are you saying that Rebecca . . . that she did it to her own cat on purpose?"

"She promised never to do it again," Piper said softly. "I think she knew it was wrong, really."

"But that's terrible!"

"Yes, I suppose it is. But at least Shellycoat survived. Her sister wasn't so lucky."

"Why, what happened to her?"

"We had two cats for a while, Shellycoat and Selkie. Rebecca had one and I had the other. Did you notice the big fireplace in the kitchen? We were in there one evening when Rebecca stood up and walked over to it, holding Selkie. I'll always remember how she just stood there, looking at the flames for the longest time and then, all of a sudden she . . . she just threw poor Selkie straight into the fire. She was so badly burnt that she didn't survive. Rebecca cried every day for a month afterwards." Piper shook her head. "God knows what possessed her to do it in the first place. That was when Dad bought me Dark Tom. Hey, why don't we walk down to Neist Point and I'll show you the lighthouse? Sometimes you can see dolphins and whales and basking sharks and all kinds of things down there."

I couldn't get the image of Selkie being burned to death out of my head. Had Rebecca really been capable of doing something so awful? I wanted to carry on talking about her, but Piper seemed to want to change the subject because as soon as I started to ask another question, she cut me off. "Have you ever been diving?" she asked. "There's lots of good diving around these cliffs because of all the wrecks and anemones and dead men's fingers and things."

"Dead men's fingers? What's that?"

"Oh, it's this stuff that looks a bit like coral, only softer and sort of swollen. It grows on the rocks. Look, there's some down there!"

We carried on walking down the path for a couple of minutes before Piper said, "I'm really sorry about what happened to your friend. Dad told us that he died just recently. It must have been such an awful shock for you. What was his name?"

"Jay," I said, and saying it aloud made a lump rise in my throat. I really didn't want to talk about him, not to Piper or anyone, but I couldn't expect Piper to talk to me about her sister if I refused to talk about my friend.

"Were the two of you a couple?" Piper asked.

"No. We'd been best friends for ages—we met at school when we were four. It was never a romantic thing. But . . ."

"But what?"

"Well . . . just a few days before he . . . he . . ." God, I just couldn't say it. I just couldn't say the word *died*. That would make it real. Being so far away in Skye I could almost pretend that Jay was still back home, waiting for me to return so that we could go to our café or hang out at the bowling alley or see a film at the cinema.

Piper was looking at me, waiting for me to go on, so I cleared my throat and tried again. "A couple of weeks ago we were at my house when he . . . he asked me if I would go to the end-of-school dance with him. I thought he was joking so I laughed. And, a moment later, he laughed too, but afterwards I thought that . . . I don't know . . . that maybe . . ."

"Maybe he was asking you for real?" Piper asked in a sympathetic voice.

"Yeah. And now I'm just . . . I worry that he was being serious and, if he was, then how could I have just laughed at him like that?"

I hadn't spoken about that awkward moment between us to anyone, had hardly even acknowledged it to myself. Tears pricked my eyes and I knew I needed to change the subject quickly or I'd end up sobbing like a little kid and wouldn't be able to stop.

In my mind, I could see him again, standing there in the dark parking lot, blowing me a kiss I'd thought was just meant to be a kind of joke.

And I heard the last words he'd ever say to me: *Anything for you . . .*

"What would you have said?" Piper asked quietly. "If he really was being serious?"

"I don't know," I replied, digging my nails into my palms. "I honestly don't know."

Piper didn't ask any more questions, and, a moment later, we suddenly came across a simple white cross at the edge of the cliff. As we got closer, I was startled to see the name printed neatly across it: REBECCA CRAIG.

"This is where she died," Piper said. "Didn't you know?"

"No. My parents never told me how it happened."

"I suppose they didn't want to upset you. It was so awful. She came out here all by herself in the middle of the night. No one knows why. It was January, there was snow everywhere, and it gets terribly windy on the island in the winter. As much as ninety miles an hour, so they say, and you'd believe it if you heard it—it howls like anything. My grandmother used to say it was the *Sluagh*, the spirits of the restless dead, traveling around the island in packs. I guess living on an island makes people very superstitious. The *Sluagh* are supposed to approach from the west, and people always say you should keep the west-facing windows of a house closed so they can't get in. God only knows what possessed Rebecca to come out here like that, all by herself in the middle of the night. She knew

74

we were absolutely forbidden from doing it. But that was typical of Rebecca, always doing something she wasn't supposed to."

"Did she fall over the cliff?"

"Yes, but that's not what killed her. She fell three meters and landed on a little rocky outcrop sticking out of the side. She broke her leg when she fell so she wasn't able to climb back up again. There was so much snow that year. None of us had any idea she was out here. It wasn't until the morning that we realized she was gone. By then she'd frozen to death."

"How horrible!"

Piper's lovely face was troubled as she gazed out across the water. "It must have been so scary for her, all alone like that. She must have called and called for help, but we were too far away to hear her. You know, sometimes, when we're at home at night, the wind out on the clifftop can play tricks on you, can almost sound like a voice. A couple of times I really thought I heard her calling my name, as if she was still lost out here, trying to find her way home." She glanced at me then and said, "Sophie, can I ask you a favor?"

"Sure. What is it?"

"Don't mention Rebecca's name back at the house. You saw how everyone reacted last night. It's just that she's such a painful subject for my family. Lilias never met her, of course, but sometimes I think she's haunted by Rebecca as much as any of us. She's terrified of her old bedroom, you know, and won't walk past it if she can help it. Mom had her nervous breakdown and Dad's had this complete obsession with gates and fences and locks ever since. I think he's worried sick that the same thing will happen to Lilias. And I'm afraid Cameron blames Rebecca for what happened to his hand. I suppose it *was* her fault—she was the one who started the fire, after all. Obviously, it would have been terrible for anyone, but because Cameron's a musician it's even worse for him. He's learned how to play the piano with just one hand, but it's not the same, and there are some pieces that he can't play at all anymore because you've just got to have two hands. It's the one thing he can't forgive her for. I don't think he ever will. You won't upset everyone by talking about Rebecca, will you?"

"I . . . I'll try not to," I said. The moment the words were out of my mouth, I regretted it.

She beamed at me. "I knew I could count on you."

FIVE

How brightly beamed her laughing eye,
As a well-known voice was heard,
And driving up to the cottage door,
Her lover's sleigh appeared.

We turned back towards the house soon after that and I took a few pictures of it from the outside before we went in.

As soon as we stepped through the front door I heard the most beautiful music I'd ever heard in my whole life. It was sweet and lilting, soft and sad, full of unspoken words and half-remembered dreams.

"Cameron obviously thought he'd sneak a bit of practice in while we were out," Piper said.

"Is that *Cameron* playing?" I asked, hardly able to believe it.

Piper smiled at me. "I told you he was good. We can go and listen if you'd like—he won't notice us walk in. He never notices anything once he starts to play. I think the whole house could be burning down around him and he'd still play to the end of the piece."

So we went into the old school hall, with its raised stage at one end. Cameron was sitting at the piano, his dark head bent over the keys as his left hand flew up and down them. I couldn't help wishing I'd been able to hear him play when he could still use both hands, but even with only one, the music was breathtaking. I felt like I could stay there and listen to him play forever.

The room was completely different during the day. Sunlight slanted in through the full-length windows, catching dust motes that danced in the beams, and shining off the smooth wooden boards of the stage.

Finally, the beautiful piece came to an end and there was just the last lingering echo as Cameron held his fingers down on the final notes. Piper immediately burst into applause and I couldn't help feeling a bit irritated with her for giving our presence away. Cameron instantly snatched his hand from the piano and his blue eyes were cold when he turned to look at us.

"Back so soon?" he said. "I thought you'd be out for longer."

"Oh, please don't let us stop you," I said. "That was wonderful."

I thought his expression softened just a little, but his voice was still cool when he said, "I'm glad you approve."

"Would you play something else?"

Cameron's hand twitched towards the keys and I thought, for a moment, he was going to agree, when Piper ruined it by saying, "Yes, please play something else, Cameron. I know, how about 'Sweet Seraphina'? That's a beautiful one and you play it so well."

"Hardly. In fact, I can't play it at all anymore," Cameron said. He stood up and closed the lid with a bang that made the keys shiver, sending out faint echoes of themselves, as if the piano itself was sighing. "That piece of music requires two hands and can't be adapted to only one."

"Oh!" Piper winced. "I'm sorry, Cameron, I didn't realize."

"Why should you?" Cameron asked, and there was ice in his voice. "You know nothing about music."

"I'm sorry, I was only trying to help."

"Trying to help!" Cameron repeated, and there was a savage bitterness in his voice I didn't understand. "I never asked for your help, Piper, and I certainly don't want it! Why aren't you two off picking berries or something? Isn't that the kind of mindless thing girls like to do? I thought I'd get an hour's peace at least, but clearly that was too much to hope for."

And with that he jumped off the stage and stalked past us.

"Oh dear," Piper said once he was gone. "I've upset him again. I told you he was sensitive about his hand." She sighed and then said brightly, "Oh, well, that's boys for you! That's why I'm so pleased you've come to stay with us. It's nice to have some girl company for a change."

We walked back out to the entrance hall, and as we went past Dark Tom's cage he started to hum. It was a weird sound and, like his speech, it made me think of a child who wasn't quite right in the head. A child shut up by himself in the dark for too long, who didn't really understand the sounds he was making and was just trying to copy something he'd heard from someone else. He bobbed his head up and down to the rhythm as he hummed, and shuffled his clawed feet up and down his perch. The song wasn't quite in tune but I would have recognized it anywhere, as it was the one that still haunted my dreams: the simple, singsong melody that had played from Jay's phone the night he died.

I stopped so abruptly beside his cage that Piper almost walked into me. "What's that tune he's humming?" I asked, and my voice came out harsher than I'd meant it to.

"How odd," Piper said, staring at Tom. "You know, he hasn't hummed that one in years and years. It was

Rebecca's favorite song. It's an old folk ballad called 'Fair Charlotte.'"

"Charlotte?"

"Yes, it's about a girl called Charlotte who goes to a ball but refuses to wear a cloak because she wants everyone to see how pretty she looks in her gown. She travels with her boyfriend, Charlie, in an open carriage, but by the time they reach the ball she's frozen to death."

Charlotte is cold . . .

The words from the Ouija-board app floated back to me and I shuddered.

"Dark Tom often hums and sings to himself when Cameron's been playing the piano, but he normally just tries to copy whatever song he last heard. I wonder if Lilias has been singing it to him?"

"Why was it Rebecca's favorite song?" I asked.

"Oh, because of the dolls, I suppose."

"What dolls?"

"The Frozen Charlotte dolls. Rebecca had a collection of them. They're based on the dead girl from the song. She just adored them."

"Could I see them?"

"If you'd like. They're in her room."

We went up the stairs, leaving the humming parrot behind us. Piper opened the door and we stepped into a room that had the dense, airless feel of a place that'd been kept shut up for too long. I instantly felt sticky and hot.

I was vaguely aware of a bed and a wardrobe and a dressing table and all the normal things a seven-year-old's bedroom would have, but the thing that instantly caught my attention was the doll display cabinet. Two meters tall, it had a glass door that allowed you to see the rows of shelves within, all lined with dolls.

After what Piper had said about the folk ballad, I'd expected the Frozen Charlotte dolls to be dressed in beautiful ball gowns, with pretty blonde ringlets on their heads, long eyelashes, and maybe elaborate hats and dainty slippers. But these dolls weren't like that. In fact, they weren't like any doll I'd ever seen before.

Made from delicate white porcelain, the Frozen Charlottes were stretched out on their backs, completely naked, with short, painted curls and a pinkish blush to their death-white cheeks. The rosebud lips were little more than a painted red dot, making the dolls look prim and disapproving somehow. Their painted eyes were all different—some were open, some were closed, and some of the dolls were so faded with age that they didn't look like they had eyes at all.

The dolls were all very small; some were no bigger than a penny and most were just a few centimeters long. A lot of them were chipped or broken in some way, missing arms or legs or even heads. Unlike normal dolls, they had no joints, so their limbs couldn't be moved. They were frozen in place, lying on their backs with their arms bent at the elbow and their hands stuck up in the air like claws, reaching for their last dying breath. Like little bodies laid out in the morgue. This wasn't Charlotte on her way to the ball—this was Charlotte after she'd died.

"But they're dead!" I blurted out.

The sight of those outstretched white hands reminded me of the cold fingers I'd felt all over my skin in my nightmare, scratching and pinching and clawing at me.

"Yes, I think they were supposed to teach kids a lesson, you know? Always wear a coat, do as your mother says, that kind of thing. Rebecca found them just after we moved in. They were downstairs in the basement. We think they must have belonged to the children when this was a school back in Edwardian times. Some of the Charlottes were in a locked box, but there wasn't room for all of them so the rest were painted into the plaster on the walls. Isn't that strange? Some kind of art project or something, I suppose. You can tell which ones were in the wall because they still have bits of plaster stuck to them. Dad chipped them out for Rebecca after she found them."

I stared again through the glass at the dolls. Most were entirely naked but a few of them had painted shoes or a painted bonnet or stockings with blue bows at the top.

Piper said, "Rebecca took one of the dolls with her. That night she sneaked out. It must have shattered when she fell over the edge of the cliff. The only thing that survived was the head. They found her holding it the next morning. I've kept it with me ever since—look." She reached beneath her T-shirt and pulled out a necklace on a silver chain. It was strung with a single Frozen Charlotte head, and what I thought were white beads at first. Then I looked closer and realized they were hands, dozens of dolls' hands, and even a couple of white arms.

"The head looked a bit odd by itself so I added some of the spare hands," Piper said. "Most of the dolls are missing limbs. I mean, they're more than a hundred years old, so it's no wonder they're a bit battered."

Personally, I thought the hands only made the necklace even stranger, but I didn't want to say so when Piper was presenting it to me so proudly.

"It's lovely," I managed.

"It makes me feel close to Rebecca," Piper said, tucking it back beneath her T-shirt. She gestured to the cabinet. "The dolls that aren't broken are worth more money. So are the ones with bonnets and stockings. And the Black Charlottes too, of course."

"Why are they all naked?"

"Children were supposed to make little outfits for them out of bits of velvet and ribbon and things. They're small so they'd only need scraps to make a dress. The Victorians used to put them into Christmas puddings as charms, and in the summer they froze the little ones and used them as ice cubes in drinks. Isn't that sweet?"

Sure, I thought, *dead dolls as ice cubes are just adorable.*

"They float on their backs in the bath too," Piper went on. "So they're called Bathing Babies. Rebecca even had a Frozen Charlotte music box." She walked over to the dressing table. "Dad found it for her in some antique shop and gave it to her one Christmas."

The box on the dressing table was completely white, with pale silver icicles stenciled on the lid. When Piper opened it, a tinkling version of the "Fair Charlotte" ballad began to play, and two small figures started to dance. I stepped forward to get a closer look at them and saw that it was Charlie and Charlotte dancing together. They both wore Victorian dress, but while Charlie's skin was pink and warm, Charlotte's was white, her lips were painted blue, and tiny snowflakes clung to her dress and hair. Charlie was dancing with a corpse.

"The dance they never had," Piper said, closing the lid with a snap. "Weren't the Victorians peculiar?"

"What are you doing?"

We turned around to see Lilias standing in the doorway, staring at us with a look of utter horror.

"I was just showing Sophie the dolls," Piper said.

"You're not going to let them out, are you?" Lilias asked, her eyes huge.

"They're staying right where they are in the cabinet, Lilias," Piper replied. "There's nothing to worry about. Look, the key is still right here in the music box."

"Dad wants you to help put lunch out," Lilias said. She kept glancing nervously at the doll cabinet.

"All right, I'll come down," Piper replied.

After she'd gone, I followed Lilias down the hall to her room.

"Can I come in?" I asked. Lilias nodded so I slipped in and said, "I'm sorry if I upset you yesterday. I really want us to be friends—we are cousins, after all."

"Cameron says we're not really cousins," Lilias said. "He says you're not even related to us and that you shouldn't have come here."

I felt my cheeks burn in a flush. "Oh. But your dad is my mom's stepbrother. So we're almost cousins, aren't we?" I sat down cross-legged on the floor so I was closer to her level and said, "You know, I agree with you—I think Rebecca's Frozen Charlotte dolls are creepy too."

Lilias looked at me but said nothing.

"Those painted dead faces are enough to scare anyone," I went on. "And I don't like how white they are. What is it that you don't like about them?"

Lilias was silent for a moment, then she looked me right in the eye and said in a challenging voice, "I don't like it when they move around at night."

Without meaning to, I raised my eyebrows.

"I knew you wouldn't believe me," Lilias said at once. "No one ever does. But they *do* move around at night. I hear them in there, scratching at the glass, trying to get out."

"Why?" I asked. "What do they want?"

Lilias folded her arms in front of her chest and glared at me. "They want to kill me. They want to kill you too. And Rebecca says she's going to let them out."

SIX

"Oh daughter dear," her mother cried,
"This blanket round you fold!
It is a dreadful night tonight,
You'll catch your death of cold."

Piper had to go to the beach with her dad after lunch—apparently he was doing a painting of her and needed to carry on while the light was right—so I took the opportunity to poke around the rest of the house a bit more while they were gone. I went into the old class-room again and looked at the black-and-white class photo. The girl with the blindfold really bothered me. I got a cold, prickly feeling all over my skin whenever I looked at her.

Finally, I pulled my attention away from the photo and wandered over to the rolltop desks. When I lifted one of the lids I found a collection of notebooks inside. I rummaged through them, hoping to find something of

Rebecca's. I wasn't disappointed. Right at the bottom of a pile of Piper's old spelling books I found a notebook with Rebecca's name on it.

I thought it was a handwriting book at first, but then when I flicked through the pages I realized it was actually a book of lines. The first four pages were covered in the same sentence written out over and over again: *I must not tell lies. I must not tell lies. I must not tell lies.*

The entire book was full of lines, all with different dates at the top of the page, copied out over and over again in Rebecca's spiky handwriting.

I must not bite my sister.

I must not be devious.

I must not say vile things.

I must not be cruel to cats.

I must not break things in temper.

I must not tear off butterflies' wings.

I must not spread unkind rumors.

I must not play with dead mice.

The terrible list went on and on. I put the disturbing book away and went back up to my room, trying to make sense of it all. It was stuffy and hot in there again and I wished I could open the window. Instead, I went and sat by it to look out at the view. The burnt tree ruined what would have otherwise been a very pretty scene. It was such a horrible sight and I wondered why Uncle James didn't have it chopped down. Lilias was out there in the garden, skipping around and around the tree in an endless circle. Watching her was making my head ache.

Finally, I decided to go outside and speak to her again, but when I got up and walked out of my bedroom she was standing at the top of the stairs.

"How . . . how did you get there so fast?" I asked, staring at her.

She gave me one of her suspicious looks. "What do you mean?"

"Weren't you just outside? By the burnt tree?"

But even as I said it I knew it couldn't have been Lilias. There was no way she could have gotten back into the house and all the way up the stairs so quickly.

"I haven't gone outside today," Lilias said. Then she added, "It was probably her."

My mouth suddenly felt very dry. "Who?"

Lilias scowled at me. "You know who," she said, and then stomped past me to her room.

I stared after her for a second before going downstairs and letting myself out into the garden. There was no girl there now. I realized that, from the window, I hadn't actually seen her face. Lilias was the same age Rebecca had been when she died, and they both had long, black hair. I thought of the girl I'd seen standing on the table in the café when it all went dark—the one who seemed to disappear as soon as the lights went on. *Could* that have been Rebecca? And if I'd seen her once, then might I have just seen her again in the garden?

Slowly, I walked over to the burnt tree. It was a foreboding thing, rising black and twisted into the air, sending a long shadow across the lawn. When I got closer I could see the ruins of the tree house. A mess of rotting black planks and scorched rope still nestled between two thick branches.

I thought of Cameron playing the piano with only his left hand and wondered whether perhaps he'd been in the tree house when the fire started.

I had a last look around the garden, half hoping to see some neighboring girl with long, dark hair that would explain the girl I'd seen skipping around the tree. But I didn't really expect to see anyone, not when the nearest house was miles away. Lilias had been inside but I *had* seen someone out here, and I was afraid I knew exactly who that person had been.

The five of us sat down to dinner that evening, just as we had the night before. Uncle James came out of his studio smelling of paint and seemed pleased with his work. I was relieved to see that Piper had made pizza for dinner so there could be no chance of Lilias finding some hidden bone and freaking out again. The meal seemed to be going well until Uncle James said, "And what have you been up to today, Lilias? I've hardly seen you."

"Playing."

"Playing? Normally you complain about having to play by yourself."

"I wasn't playing by myself."

"Who were you playing with then?"

"With Rebecca."

There was a sudden dead silence around the table. Everyone was staring at Lilias.

Uncle James took a deep breath. "Lilias," he said. "We've talked about this. I will not be lied to. One minute it's dolls running around the place with knives and now it's Rebecca. It's got to stop."

"But I'm not lying!"

"You know perfectly well that your sister is dead. She died before you were born. So you could not possibly have been playing with her today."

"Sophie saw her too!" Lilias said, to my dismay. "She told me she saw her out by the dead tree. Didn't you?" Now everyone was looking at me. "I . . . I did think I saw a girl in the garden," I said. "I thought it was Lilias at first but—"

Cameron slammed his fork down on the table so suddenly that the sound made me jump. "Are we really going to have this conversation?" he asked. "Even if there was a girl in the garden, it clearly could not have been Rebecca."

"But I did play with her today!" Lilias said. "She likes me because we're the same age. She says I'm her favorite sister."

"Lilias, I don't want to have to start taking you to Dr. Phillips twice a week again, but if you carry on with these astonishing lies then you'll be straight down there for a session first thing in the morning."

Lilias stood up and stomped her foot hard on the floor. "I am *not* a liar!" she said, and her voice came out a shriek. "All I ever do is tell the truth and get punished for it! I'm never telling you the truth again, ever!"

And then she ran from the room without another word. Cameron half rose from his seat, as if to go after her, but Uncle James said, "Just leave her. The last thing she needs right now is extra attention." Cameron slowly sat back down, but he didn't look very happy about it.

Uncle James pinched the bridge of his nose. He suddenly looked very tired. "I'm sorry about this, Sophie," he said. "I don't know what you must think of us all. It's been very hard on Lilias, growing up without her mother around."

I nodded, feeling embarrassed. "There . . . was a girl in the garden, though," I began uncertainly, feeling like I ought to say something in Lilias's defense.

"I don't see how," Cameron said shortly. "None of the local children ever come up here. And, even if they had, they wouldn't have been able to get into the garden. The gate is always kept locked, remember?"

He looked so irritated that I dropped the subject. After dinner I offered to help clean up, but Piper wouldn't let me, so I decided to go to bed. I was halfway up the stairs when Cameron caught up with me.

"Sophie, can I talk to you for a moment?"

Since he'd mostly avoided me since I arrived, I was surprised to find him seeking me out now, but I said, "Of course."

As usual, his right hand stayed buried in his pocket, and his blue eyes had that piercing look as if they could see right inside my head.

"Are you really going to stay here for the whole two weeks?" he asked.

The question took me aback. "Er . . . that's the plan," I said.

"Isn't there anyone else you can stay with while your parents are away?"

"Why?"

"This house is . . . well, you can see that we have our issues. It's not good for you to be here. You shouldn't have come."

"I'm sorry you feel like that," I said stiffly. "I'll try to stay out of your way."

I turned and would have continued up the stairs, but he grabbed hold of my arm. "Sophie, please. I'm not . . . I'm only trying to warn you—" He broke off abruptly.

"Warn me of what?" I asked. "You don't think the dolls are haunted too, do you?"

"Dolls? What dolls?" He looked genuinely baffled.

"The Frozen Charlotte dolls," I said. "Lilias thinks they're haunted or something."

"Of course I don't think the dolls are haunted!" Cameron said impatiently. "Lilias is half out of her mind with fear. You must have realized that by now? The last thing she needs is you feeding all of her phobias and paranoia."

"Well, what are you trying to warn me about, then?"

He let go of my arm. "Never mind," he said. "Just forget I said anything."

"How am I supposed to do that?" I said. "Why do you have to be so mysterious about it, whatever it is?"

But I knew it was useless—he wasn't going to say anything, nothing sensible anyway. He just stood and looked at me with his jaw clamped firmly shut. The paleness of his skin emphasized his cheekbones and made his dark hair seem coal-black—he was very handsome, in a cold sort of way. I could imagine what Jay would have had to say about him if he'd met him. His voice was clear inside my head: *He looks like he should be wearing a necktie and storming around the moors in the rain, shouting about something.*

Before I could stop myself, I laughed. Then I realized what I'd done and clapped my hand over my mouth, but it was too late. Oh God, I really was losing it. Even though Jay was dead, I was still laughing at his jokes.

Cameron stared at me. "I'm sorry, have I said something funny?"

I shook my head, lowered my hand, and tried to pull myself together. "No," I said. "No, I can't imagine you ever saying something funny."

Cameron raised an eyebrow. "You think I've got no sense of humor."

It was a statement rather than a question.

Great, I thought. *Now I've offended him too.*

"I don't know," I said, desperately trying to think of the right words. "I mean, we don't really know each other."

"No," he replied. "No, we don't."

Then he just walked past me and up the stairs without another word.

"Never do that again!" Dark Tom said suddenly downstairs. *"Never do that again!"*

"Quiet, Tom!" I said as firmly as I could. "I want to try to get some sleep tonight."

The parrot tilted his head and stared at me through the bars, but didn't say anything more. I went up to my room, got changed, and went to bed. The wind had started up again outside, blowing its way around the house and rattling the windows in their frames. I tried not to think about what Piper had said about the *Sluagh*, but that howling sound made it easy to believe the spirits of the restless dead were out there, circling the house, looking for a way in . . .

That night, I dreamed about Jay. He was sitting next to me in our math class. We were in the middle of an exam and I was letting him copy my answers when suddenly he leaned over and whispered in my ear, "I have a present for you."

Then he put a white box on the table and opened the lid. A tinkling melody began to play and I recognized the tune at once—it was the "Fair Charlotte" ballad. Two figures danced together in the music box and, when I looked closely, I could see they were Jay and me. The tiny figure of Jay had water dripping off it and the little figure of me looked normal to begin with, but when I peered at it more closely I saw that my skin was white, there were icicles clinging to my dress, and tiny drops of blood dripped from my fingers onto Jay's hands.

I gasped and drew back from the music box.

"What's the matter?" Jay asked, sounding hurt. "Don't you like it?"

I turned to look at him and saw that he was soaking wet. Water ran down his face from his hair, and his school uniform was drenched.

"You're . . . You're soaking wet!" I said.

"Well, I drowned, Sophie," he said, sounding irritated. "What did you expect?"

He sounded almost more like Cameron than Jay and, even as I had the thought, it was suddenly Cameron sitting there at the desk, dripping wet just like he'd been the night I arrived at the house. "It's not safe for you here," he said, scowling at me. "It's not safe for any of us."

He reached out towards the music box with a hand that was horribly burnt and shoved it across the table towards me. It fell into my lap and blood poured out of it, staining my hands and skirt, running down my legs and filling up my shoes. And the whole time that tinkling tune continued to play, over and over again, scraping away at the inside of my head, peeling little broken pieces off my heart . . .

I gave a muffled shriek and jerked awake in my bed, my heart hammering in my chest. The "Fair Charlotte" song was still playing and, at first, I thought it was just inside my head, a horrid shard of the nightmare still lodged in my brain. But then I realized that I really was hearing the song, that it was the tinkling tune of the music box and it was coming from Rebecca's room, which meant that someone had opened the lid and was in there, right now, in the middle of the night.

SEVEN

"Oh no, oh no!" Fair Charlotte cried,
And she laughed like a gypsy queen.
"To ride in blankets muffled up,
I never would be seen!"

It was such a soft sound that if I hadn't been in the room right next door I never would have heard it. But it came to me clearly through the wall and I knew it meant that someone had opened the music box lid. I glanced at my phone and saw that it was after midnight.

Feeling cold all over, I swung my legs over the side of the bed and stood up. Snatching up the flashlight I'd found in the bedside drawer, I tiptoed out to the corridor but didn't turn the flashlight on. If someone was out there, I didn't want to warn them I was coming.

As soon as I stepped out onto the landing, the tune became clearer, and I saw at once that Rebecca's door was slightly ajar. It had definitely been closed when I'd come to bed. There was no light shining through the crack, just pitch-black and that hateful little tune spilling out of the darkness. Part of me wanted to run back to my room, jump under the covers, and hide there until daylight. But I had to find out what was going on, for Jay's sake.

I crept softly over to the door, the flashlight shaking in my hand. Silently, I counted to three and then quickly shoved the door open and slapped my hand against the wall, but although I ran my fingers frantically all around, I couldn't find a light switch, so I snapped on the flashlight and jerked it this way and that around the room.

First the bed swung into view in the beam of light, then the doll cabinet up against the wall and then, finally, the dressing table with the music box sitting open on it, the little figures of Charlotte and Charlie twirling around and around in their endless dance. It was awful not being able to see the entire room at once. Shadows moved around the beam as I swept it around the room once, twice, three times. There was no trace of anyone there. The room seemed to be empty.

I walked over to the dressing table and reached out and closed the music box lid with a snap. The tune cut off at once.

And that was when I heard the scratching.

It was coming from the doll cabinet behind me. A frantic *scratch, scratch, scratch*, as if hundreds of tiny fingers were scrabbling and scraping over glass.

I whirled on the spot and jerked my flashlight towards the doll cabinet.

When the light hit them, I almost dropped the flashlight in shock.

The dolls were all still and silent on their shelves, but they weren't lying down like they'd been before. Now every single one of them was standing up and facing out, their tiny hands resting against the glass, their painted eyes all staring directly at me. Even the ones missing a leg or an arm or a head were pressed up against the door, facing out of the cabinet.

At that moment a small hand crept into mine, cold fingers wrapping around my own, just like that night at the café. I gasped, my heart racing in my chest, and snatched my hand away, while instinctively striking out with the hand holding the flashlight. It made contact with the small shape beside me in the dark, and there was a grunt and a thump.

I shone the flashlight in front of me and saw a little girl with long, dark hair sprawled on the floor. For a second I thought it was Rebecca, but then I saw that the huge, frightened eyes belonged to Lilias. One hand was pressed to her cheek where I'd hit her but, before I could say anything, she scrambled back to her feet, gripped my hand, and practically dragged me from the room and down the corridor to her own bedroom. Her bedside lamp was on, creating a soft, warm glow.

"I'm so sorry, Lilias," I said, squeezing her shaking hand. "I didn't mean to hit you. Are you okay?"

Lilias snatched her hand from mine and glared at me. I could see that her cheek was red where I'd hit her, but I hadn't broken the skin. She was trembling from head to foot. And at the top of her nightgown I could clearly see the terrible, ugly scar running across her collarbone where she had tried to cut it out.

"How can you be so stupid?" she said, still glaring. "You shouldn't ever go in Rebecca's room. If you let the dolls out, they'll do bad things."

"I wasn't going to let them out," I said. "I heard the music box and wanted to see if someone was in the room."

"Rebecca was there," Lilias said. "In the corner— didn't you see her? She wants to show you the dolls. You saw them move, didn't you? You heard them scratching at the glass?"

"I . . . I thought I heard something," I said. "But why would Rebecca want to show me the dolls?"

"Why don't you ask her?" Lilias said fiercely. "You're the one who brought her here."

"But I can't see her. Not properly. Lilias, are you really

saying you can see Rebecca? That you've actually spoken to her?"

I remembered what Lilias had said that night at the dinner table: *She likes me because we're the same age . . .*

It was true—Rebecca had been seven years old when she died, the same age Lilias was now. They even looked kind of similar.

"She's here," Lilias whispered. "And she's really, really angry."

"Why?" I asked. "What's she angry about?"

But Lilias just shook her head and refused to say anything more about Rebecca. "Next time you hear the dolls moving around in the night," she said, "just close your eyes and pretend you can't hear them. That's what I do. It's no use telling anyone because no one will believe you. No one ever believes you, especially not Dad. He'll just get angry and call you a liar."

I tried asking her about Rebecca a couple more times, but Lilias just pursed her lips and shook her head so, in the end, I decided to give up and go to bed.

I said good-night and was almost at the door when Lilias said, "You didn't bring any needles with you, did you?"

"Needles? No. Why?"

"I was just going to tell you to hide them," Lilias said. "To hide anything that's sharp. That's what the Frozen Charlottes will look for if they get out of the cabinet."

"Needles? But why?"

"To poke out your eyes while you're asleep. That's what they do. That's what they did to that blindfolded girl in the school photo. That's why the grown-ups had the dolls plastered into the walls. But then Rebecca found them and let them all out."

When I went down to breakfast the next morning, Uncle James was already working in his studio, but Piper and Cameron were at the dining room table with cereal bowls and glasses of juice.

I pulled out a chair and sat down just as Lilias walked into the room. I was horrified to see that an ugly purple bruise had formed around her cheek on the spot where I'd accidentally hit her last night. Her eyes met mine, but she didn't say anything as she walked over and sat down with us.

"I'm catching the bus into town this afternoon, Lilias," Cameron said as he scooped up a spoonful of cornflakes. "I thought maybe you'd like to come with me and we could go to the sweet shop. What do you—?" He glanced at Lilias and stopped mid-sentence—he'd clearly noticed her bruised cheek. The spoon froze in his hand and he went rigid all over. "What happened to your face?" he asked in a voice that was suddenly hoarse.

I opened my mouth to confess, but before I could utter a single word, Lilias said, "I just fell. That's all."

What happened next took place so fast that I almost couldn't take it in. Cameron's chair screeched across the floor as he leaped to his feet, dragged Piper from her chair, and slammed her hard up against the wall.

"What did you do?" he asked in a voice that was horribly quiet.

"Nothing," she gasped. "I haven't done anything."

"It was me!" I said, already out of my chair. "For God's sake, it was me!" I clamped my hand around Cameron's arm and tried to pull him away from Piper, but his grip was like a vice and I could feel all the muscle and sinew straining in his forearm. He turned to look at me, his eyes icy-cold.

"Cameron, you're hurting me," Piper whimpered. Without moving his gaze from mine, Cameron finally let her go and she quickly stepped away from him, rubbing at both her arms.

"You?" Cameron snapped. "What do you mean it was you?"

"It was a mistake," I said. "Last night. I went to—"

"She went to the bathroom," Lilias said. "And I made her jump in the corridor. She hit me with her flashlight. It was an accident."

"An accident?" Cameron had gone pale and seemed to be looking through me rather than at me.

"Yes," I said. "It was just an accident. I'm sorry."

Cameron's eyes focused on me suddenly. He took a sharp step back. "Be more careful in the future," he snapped. "We've had enough accidents in this house."

And with that he turned and stormed off, slamming the door hard behind him.

"He's mad," I said, still shaken by what I'd just seen. "What's wrong with him?"

"Nothing," Piper said. Her sea-green eyes were filled with tears. "Nothing. He just gets a bit worked up sometimes, that's all. He can't help it."

"Of course he can help it!" I said. "Does your dad know he can get violent like this?"

"It's not a big deal," Piper said, rubbing at her bruised arms. "Please just forget it."

I thought of nothing else for the rest of that morning. At lunchtime, Uncle James joined us and it felt so strange sitting around the table with Cameron and Piper acting quite normally towards each other after what had happened earlier. When Cameron asked her to pass the salt he spoke as if they'd never had any disagreement at all, as if he hadn't attacked her just a few hours before.

"I'm catching the bus into Dunvegan later," Cameron

announced to the table in general. "Lilias is coming with me to go to the sweet shop. I thought perhaps Sophie might like to tag along and see the town?"

His invitation startled me, and I quickly tried to turn him down. "Oh, I don't think that I—"

But Uncle James cut me off. "That sounds like a great idea."

"I'll come with you too," Piper said brightly.

"No, I need you here," Uncle James said. "You're sitting for me this afternoon, remember?"

"Oh, but Dad, couldn't I—"

"Sorry, Piper, but I really need to finish this painting. The gallery is waiting for it."

"Good. So it's all settled then," Cameron said, glancing at me. "We'll leave after lunch."

Piper looked unhappy, and I probably looked much the same, but there didn't seem to be any way out of it and, a short while later, I was walking to the bus stop with Cameron and Lilias. It was a twenty minute bus journey and, throughout that time, I didn't speak to Cameron and he didn't say one word to me; he just slouched with his hands in his pockets, staring out the window in silence. I couldn't understand why he'd suggested that I come in the first place.

When we arrived in town, Lilias headed straight for the sweet shop—it was an old-fashioned kind of place, with shelves lined with big glass jars filled with sweets of all different shapes and colors. Cameron handed Lilias a striped paper bag and I lingered awkwardly while she ran around filling it up.

Cameron took another bag and then, to my surprise, turned to me and said, "What would you like? My treat."

"Oh, I don't want anything," I said, flustered. "I'll just wait outside."

I couldn't understand why Cameron was being nice. It was like he'd suddenly turned into a different person.

I was even more confused when he came out of the shop a few minutes later and pressed a paper bag into my hand. "Here," he said. "Since you wouldn't say what you wanted, I had to guess. You strike me as a sugar mice kind of girl."

I stared at the bag in my hand, filled with pink and white sugar mice. They were, in fact, my favorite and it irritated me that Cameron had been able to guess. Almost as if those piercing eyes of his really could see inside my head.

"I hate sugar mice," I lied, stuffing the bag in my pocket.

The corner of Cameron's mouth twisted up in a half smile and I was sure he knew I was lying. Lilias came out of the shop then and we started to walk back down the path.

"What's your deal, anyway?" I asked. "It's like you've got split-personality disorder or something."

I reasoned he could hardly attack me while we were out in public but, to my surprise, he laughed instead, a loud, breathless sort of laugh that almost burst out of him and made some nearby people turn to stare.

"What's so funny?" I asked.

Cameron shook his head, and a few dark strands of hair fell into his eyes. "Not funny," he said. "Just ironic."

He didn't elaborate and we carried on walking in silence for a few minutes before he said, "I thought perhaps you'd like to see the art gallery while we're here. They buy most of Dad's paintings. Some of them will be on display."

"Sure," I said. I had the weird feeling that all of this was leading up to something, but I didn't know what.

When we arrived at the gallery, Lilias complained that the paintings were boring, so we left her sitting on a bench in the foyer, eating her sweets. Cameron led the way to the section where his dad's paintings were on display. Most of them were sea themed and the green and blue paint of the ocean really made you think you could smell the salt and hear the surf and feel the sand between your toes. I recognized one of the paintings of the lighthouse at Neist Point, and another of the beach outside the house, with its steep cliffs and black sand.

"What do you think of this one?" Cameron asked in a casual voice, pointing at one of the paintings.

It was Piper in a beach scene, only Uncle James hadn't painted her as a girl, but as a mermaid. With hundreds of tiny brushstrokes, he'd captured her perfect features and green eyes, waves of glossy, strawberry blonde hair falling loose down her back as she sat on one of the shiny black rocks rising up out of the water at the base of the lighthouse, gazing out to sea with her mermaid's fin curled beneath her. I could see the shine on each scale, see the breeze softly moving her hair and the salt spray sparkling on her skin. I was reminded of when I'd first seen Piper when I arrived at the house and had thought there was something almost mermaid-like about her beauty.

"It's amazing," I said.

"Mmm. Dad first painted Piper as a mermaid about a year ago. It was his most popular painting and it sold in a day for twice what the others had. Since then there's been a steady demand for more. You could say the mermaid paintings are our bread and butter now."

"It suits her," I said.

"Yes, I think so," Cameron replied. "Piper was delighted, of course, when Dad first painted her like that. It appealed to her sense of vanity. But I've always thought it was a curious choice—to paint your own daughter as a monster."

"Monster?"

"Of course. Mermaids are sea predators. Scavengers. Killers. They sing to lure ships to their doom on the rocks. They're said to drag sailors down under the water, drowning them and feeding off their souls."

As usual, the mention of drowning made me shiver. *Please,* I wanted to say. *Please, please don't say that word to me.* I didn't want to hear about it, or think about it, not ever again.

"I'm sure your dad didn't mean the painting that way," I managed.

Cameron looked at me. "I saw another painting of his once. One that he didn't sell to the gallery. I don't think he meant for me to see it—we've never spoken of it—and I know that Piper's certainly never seen it. He drew her as a mermaid again but, instead of sitting on the rocks, this time she was dragging a man down into the sea. She was drowning him and the expression on her face was . . . hungry, happy—she looked like a monster."

I didn't say anything, not at all sure I believed that there even was such a painting.

"He won't hear it from me," Cameron went on, almost to himself, "but when I saw that painting I thought that he must . . . he must at least suspect. At least on some level . . ." He glanced at me then and said, "I can't believe I was so stupid this morning. I played right into her hands by blaming her for what happened to Lilias. It's what she's wanted since you arrived—to show me in a bad light, to make me seem like the dangerous one."

"Why should she want to do that?" I asked.

Cameron looked back at the painting. "Piper has two faces. She's only shown you one so far but she'll show you the other soon enough. She likes people to see it eventually because it shocks them and she enjoys shocking people. You must be careful."

"What are you talking about?" I said, starting to feel impatient. "Piper has been nothing but nice to me since the moment I arrived. She's tried so hard to make me feel at home here."

"Piper is . . . not what you think," Cameron said in a careful tone. "You shouldn't take her at face value." He paused, then said slowly, "I know it looked bad this morning, the way I reacted at breakfast. But you have to understand that the relationship between Piper and me is . . . it's complicated."

"That's no excuse for attacking her," I said. "There's never any excuse for physically attacking someone like that."

Cameron looked at me sharply. "Oh, but there is," he said. "Sometimes you have to do it. Sometimes it's necessary."

I just shook my head. I couldn't help thinking of Jay. In all the years I'd known him, I'd never once seen him lash out at another person, never seen him behave violently towards anybody, never felt at all afraid or unsure around him. He was better than that, better than Cameron.

"Can we head back now?" I said. "I really don't want to talk about Piper anymore."

I thought he might argue but instead he just sighed and said, "Yes, Sophie, we can go back now. Whatever you want."

We went back out to the foyer, collected Lilias, and returned to the house.

EIGHT

My silken cloak is quite enough,
You know 'tis lined throughout.
Besides, I have my silken scarf,
To twine my neck about.

When we got back, Cameron and Lilias headed upstairs and I was about to follow them when Cameron turned around halfway up and said, "If you still don't believe me about the mermaid painting, why don't you go and say hello to my father? See for yourself what he's been working on the last couple of days."

Before I could reply, he turned and carried on up the stairs. I stood there for a moment before deciding to take him up on his suggestion. I'd hardly seen Uncle James since I arrived and the only time we'd really spoken had been when he picked me up from the ferry. I went straight to his studio and knocked on the door.

When he called for me to come in, I stepped into a bright, airy room that smelled of paint and turpentine. Uncle James sat behind an easel in the corner with his sleeves rolled up, and looked surprised to see me, almost as if he'd forgotten I was staying with them.

"Oh, Sophie," he said. "Hello. Are you back already?"

"We just arrived. Cameron showed me some of your paintings in the art gallery. I thought they were wonderful."

"Thank you."

"Is that the painting of Piper? Can I see it?"

I started to walk forward, but he instantly sprang up from his seat and moved to put himself between me and the easel. Then, almost as an afterthought, he laughed, but it sounded strained.

"Sorry," he said. "It's an artist thing. I don't like anyone to see my unfinished paintings. I'm sure you understand. So, how was town? Cameron's been making himself pleasant, I hope?"

"Everyone's been really nice."

"I'm sure Piper has loved having you around," Uncle James replied. I noticed he still had a paintbrush in his hand. The bristles were dipped in sea-green paint and, as I watched, a big droplet fell from the end to stain the already paint-splattered floor, but Uncle James didn't seem to notice. "It's nice for her to have someone her own age around. We're so isolated up here."

"It must have been hard for her, losing Rebecca like that," I said.

"Hard . . . yes. Yes, it was hard," Uncle James said. All of a sudden he seemed to look through me rather than at me, just like when he'd picked me up at the ferry. "Hard for all of us." He focused on me again and smiled. "I suppose all families have their ups and downs. We're no different."

That seemed a bit of an understatement, but I didn't say anything. Uncle James added, "We've been through a lot, but we're all right now. I know you're an only child so we probably seem quite strange to you. Perhaps you've noticed that Piper and Cameron can be a bit . . . well, just a bit hostile to each other sometimes. But they're good friends underneath it all. It's just normal sibling rivalry. Your mother and I were the same when we were kids."

I wanted to ask him whether he'd ever lunged at my mom across the breakfast table and slammed her up against a wall the way I'd seen Cameron do to Piper this morning, but it was pretty obvious that he had no idea what was really going on between them. Suddenly, I felt like he didn't have much idea about a lot of things.

Before I could say anything, the door opened and Piper stuck her head in. "Oh, there you are!" she said brightly. "I've made us some little lemon cakes. I thought we could play the tea-party game out in the garden. I made some lemonade too—it's such a hot day!"

"Splendid idea!" Uncle James said, just a little bit too eagerly. It was obvious that he was dying to get rid of me. "It's too nice a day to be stuck indoors. You girls go and have fun."

I didn't have much choice but to follow Piper outside to where she'd set out a little table, complete with a crisp white tablecloth. On it sat a jug of fresh lemonade filled with ice cubes, condensation still running down the glass, and a plate of some of the prettiest iced lemon cakes I'd ever seen.

"I only sat briefly for Dad in the end, before the light changed or something, so I had time to make these. I hope you like lemon!"

Actually, I hated it, but I couldn't exactly say so when Piper had gone to all that trouble.

"I love it," I said, trying to sound convincing. As I went to sit down I felt the rustle of the paper bag holding the sugar mice in my pocket and couldn't help wishing that Piper had been as good at guessing my favorite as Cameron had. I took the bag out of my pocket to stop the sweets from getting squished and placed it on the grass beside my chair.

I also wished Piper had picked a different spot. The burnt tree loomed above us, casting stark shadows across our white table. From where I sat I could smell the charcoal coating on the crumbling bark and, even as I watched, I saw a fine puff of ash moved by the warm breeze blow directly into the jug of lemonade.

Piper didn't seem to notice and poured a glass for me, the ice cubes clinking together in the jug. Only once she poured it I realized they weren't ice cubes at all—they were tiny Frozen Charlottes, floating on their backs like white corpses. "I borrowed some from Rebecca's collection," Piper said. "They've been in the freezer all morning so they're nice and cold. Aren't they quaint?"

It wasn't the word I would have used for the tiny dolls floating in our lemonade, with their little dead hands stretched out before them.

"I squeezed the lemons fresh this afternoon!" Piper said, smiling that dazzling smile.

And maybe it was only because of those things Cameron had said, but I found myself thinking, *Who does that?* Who makes their own lemonade from scratch? Aside from the burnt tree and the flecks of ash sitting on top of the drink, the whole scene suddenly seemed too idyllic, and somehow artificial, as if I had wandered onto the set of a play. It was the same strange feeling I'd had the first night we had dinner at the house. Even Piper's smile looked not right—too perfect and pretty to be real.

Even as I had the thought, the smile faltered on her face. "Is something wrong?" she asked.

"No, of course not," I said, quickly reaching for a cake to give my hands something to do. "I'm just . . . touched that you've gone to so much trouble."

"Oh, it's no trouble at all," Piper said. "I just want us to be friends."

"We are," I said, but it occurred to me that Piper and I didn't know each other, not really.

"Well, aren't you going to try the cake?" Piper asked.

I quickly bit into it and had to force myself not to grimace. It was way too tart and practically made my eyes water.

"It's delicious," I said, forcing myself to swallow it.

"So, how was town?" Piper asked as she poured herself some lemonade. And then, before I could answer, "What did you and Cameron talk about?" Her tone remained casual but I suddenly felt sure she knew *exactly* what Cameron and I had talked about. Whatever weird sibling rivalry was going on here, I didn't know how I'd managed to plant myself right in the middle of it.

"Nothing much." I shrugged. "I don't know why he asked me along, really."

"Well, that's a relief anyway," Piper said. "I was worried he might have taken the opportunity to pour poison into your ear."

"What do you mean?"

"Cameron doesn't like me to have friends," Piper said slowly. "It's part of his possessive nature, I think. I used to be quite popular but he's chased away most of my school friends now."

"You mean, he lies about you?"

"Yes. At least . . . well, he normally just sticks to lying."

"Normally? You mean he sometimes does more than that?"

I hadn't meant the disbelieving tone to creep into my voice, but I think it did nonetheless and Piper noticed. She looked at me and said, "You could say that. A couple of months ago, Cameron flogged my boyfriend and said that if he ever came near me again he'd get much worse. I haven't seen him since." I stared at Piper in silence for a moment.

"Flogged?" I finally managed. "You mean with a . . . with a—"

"With a riding crop," Piper said. "Ask him about it, if you don't believe me. I knew Cameron didn't like me seeing Brett but I never dreamed he'd turn violent like that. He arrived in the middle of this party we'd gone to and said he was taking me home. I didn't want to go but he grabbed my arm and dragged me out and when Brett tried to follow us Cameron hit him with the crop. It was

Lilias's—she has riding lessons once a week. Cameron brought it with him. That was the thing that disturbed me the most afterwards, I think. He'd brought it with him from home, so he must have planned to attack Brett all along." She rubbed her temples with her fingers and said, "It was so terrible. Poor Brett. He could hardly walk afterwards and the back of his shirt was all ripped and covered in blood."

"But why?" I said, suddenly feeling very cold despite the sun shining down on us. "Why did he do it?"

"I told you, he's possessive," Piper said. "He's always been like that. Even when I was a kid. And it got a lot worse after Rebecca died. He thinks he can control everyone and everything. He wants to keep me here in this house for the rest of my days. He won't go away to music college, you know, even though any college in the country would be delighted to have him, in spite of his injury. He was furious with me for dating Brett and I suppose he wanted to punish me for it."

I remembered what Cameron had said earlier about violence sometimes being necessary and felt the cold prickle of revulsion creep over my skin.

"But if he did that to your boyfriend, how can you stand to be around him?" I said. "How can you even look at him?"

"Perhaps Rebecca dying unhinged him a little." Piper sighed. "Perhaps it unhinged all of us. But you mustn't think badly of Cameron because of what I've told you. That's the last thing I want. You won't act any differently around him, will you?"

"I'll try not to," I said, and took a gulp of my lemonade.

And then something bit the inside of my mouth. Hard. I felt sharp little teeth that were not my own tearing at the inside of my cheek. The soft flesh ripped and blood poured into my mouth.

I shrieked, spitting out fat globs of blood that spotted the white tablecloth. Frantically, I reached my fingers into my mouth, grabbed hold of the thing, and flung it down on the table.

It was one of the Frozen Charlotte dolls, her white porcelain skin stained and smeared with blood. It was still dribbling from between my lips and down my chin—it felt like a great chunk of my mouth had been torn away. I even thought I felt a lump of flesh disappearing down my throat as I instinctively swallowed.

"Oh God, Sophie, are you okay?" Piper said, jumping to her feet.

"It . . . It bit me!" I exclaimed. My voice came out thick and each word caused the loose flap of skin inside my mouth to sting horribly. Blood sprayed out of my mouth when I spoke so I clapped my hand over it.

"What did?" Piper asked, staring.

"It . . . It felt like something bit me," I said, wiping the blood from my face with trembling fingers. How could I possibly say that I thought a doll had bitten me? It sounded mental, even to me.

"You must have bitten your cheek," Piper said.

Of course that was the most rational explanation—I'd bitten myself—and already I found myself starting to wonder . . . It seemed so crazy to think that that tiny white doll on the table between us had actually bitten me. She didn't even have teeth, just a painted red dot where her mouth ought to be.

"I guess so," I said.

Tentatively, I prodded the spot with my tongue. It stung like anything. I glanced down and saw that I'd managed to get a few spots of blood on my white T-shirt too. "I'd better go and change," I said. I got up and started to walk back to the house.

"Sophie," Piper said behind me. When I turned back she was holding a striped paper bag, a strange expression on her face. "You forgot your sugar mice."

"Oh. Thanks." I went back for them and then walked across the garden to the house, aware of Piper's eyes on me the whole time. It was only a bag of sugar mice. I hadn't asked Cameron to get them for me. So why did I feel a weird twist of guilt in my stomach, as if I'd somehow done something wrong?

I went upstairs to my room, took off the white T-shirt, and grabbed a clean one. I was just pulling it over my head when I heard someone giggle. It was muffled and high-pitched, girlish and strange, and my first thought was that it was Dark Tom, giggling in his cage downstairs. But then someone said my name, in fact they whispered it, and it wasn't one person, it was several, all whispering my name over and over again:

"Sophie, Sophie, Sophie . . ."

"Sophie, Sophie . . ."

"Sophie, Sophie, Sophie, Sophie . . ."

Tiny, tiny, inhuman little voices that made creeping fear travel all the way through me, right to the very end of my cold, clammy fingertips.

They were coming from Rebecca's room.

NINE

Her bonnet and her gloves were on,
She stepped into the sleigh,
Rode swiftly down the mountainside,
And over the hills away.

I pressed my ear against the wall and heard them whispering.

"Sophie . . ."

"Sophie . . ."

"Open the door, Sophie . . ."

"Let us out . . ."

"Sophie, please. Unlock the door . . ."

"Please open the door . . ."

"We want to play with you . . ."

I thought I heard crying too but then I realized it wasn't crying—it was giggling.

"Let's play the Knife Murder Game!"

"No, no, the Stick-a-Needle-in-Your-Eye Game!"

"Let's play the Push-Teacher-Down-the-Stairs Game!"

I rushed out into the corridor and threw open the door to Rebecca's room.

The voices all stopped at the exact same moment.

I stepped into the room and my eyes went straight to the doll cabinet. When I'd first seen them they'd all been lying down, and last night they were all standing up. This time, they were all lying down on the shelves again, except the ones without any heads. Those were standing up against the glass, as if they were trying to see out, even though they were headless and no longer had eyes to see with.

I walked up to the cabinet, glad of the sunlight filling the room—at least I could see them properly this time. I peered at the glass and, now that I was looking closely, I could make out the scratches. They were small and faint but they were there, crisscrossing angrily over and over one another. When I put my fingers against the glass it was smooth, which had to mean that the scratches had been made from the inside . . .

"I hear them in there," Lilias had said, *"scratching at the glass, trying to get out . . ."*

I leaned closer to the cabinet, my eyelashes almost brushing the glass as I tried to get a closer look. The Frozen Charlotte dolls who still had their arms were all bent at the elbow, their hands outstretched, tiny white fingers splayed out. And some of them had red stains around their fingernails, stains that almost looked like blood . . .

"Sophie?" Piper's voice behind me made me jump. "What are you doing?"

I jumped back guiltily. Piper didn't look angry but I still felt like a snoop being caught alone in Rebecca's room like this. "Oh, I was just . . . looking at the dolls. I hope you don't mind?"

"Of course not. They are quite fascinating, aren't they? So old. Think of all the little girls who have played with them over the years."

I saw that she had the tiny Frozen Charlotte dolls with her that she'd used as ice cubes and, as I watched, she unlocked the cabinet and put them back with the others.

"Piper, can I ask you something?"

"Of course."

"The Frozen Charlottes . . . I'm not really sure how to put this, but—"

"Uh-oh, has Lilias been telling you that they talk to her?" Piper locked the cabinet and put the key back in the music box. "She got the idea from Rebecca, you know. Somehow she must have found out that Rebecca said the dolls talked to her. I don't know if she really believed it or not, but I doubt it. I think Rebecca just used them as an excuse. Whenever she did something wrong, she would blame the dolls. If a vase got broken, or a toy went missing, or . . . that day we found Shellycoat covered in blood and . . . and the night she threw Selkie into the fire . . . She blamed the Frozen Charlotte dolls for everything. She said they were always telling her to do bad things."

"And you never thought it could be true?"

"Of course not." Piper laughed. "Dolls don't talk, do they?"

"I heard someone calling my name a moment ago," I said.

"That was probably me. I wanted to make sure you were okay."

"But it sounded like it was coming from this room. And it wasn't one voice, it was a whole bunch of them, all whispering my name at the same time."

Piper laid her hand on my arm and said gently, "I wouldn't worry about it. That sort of thing is only to be expected in your . . . well, your delicate mental state."

"I don't have a delicate mental state," I snapped, shaking her hand off irritably.

Piper sighed. "Look, Sophie, you've been through a terrible time recently. Losing your best friend like that, I mean. It's only just happened and grief can do strange things to you." She gave a small, sad laugh and said, "I should know. Remember how I told you that I used to think I could hear Rebecca crying and calling out my name on the clifftop? One time in the living room I even thought I heard hands beating at the window panes." She paused, then added, "And there were white fingers once, pressing against the glass, bloodless and covered in ice . . ." She shook her head and said, "It's probably just your brain trying to deal with what you've been through, to make sense of losing Jay like that. Lilias probably planted the idea in your mind when she told you about the Frozen Charlottes."

"I guess so," I said, but only to keep her happy. I *knew* I'd heard voices coming from Rebecca's room. They'd been real. I wasn't going crazy. Was I?

"I'd better go and get started on dinner," Piper said, giving my arm a squeeze.

"Do you want some help?"

"No, it's fine. You just relax."

When I went downstairs a few minutes later, I heard the soft strains of piano music, so pure and lovely, and when I walked into the old school hall I saw Cameron sitting at the piano on the stage.

As I listened, I felt all the things Piper had told me about him melting away. I felt the scene from this morning, where he had lunged at her so horribly, being wiped out as if it had never happened, as if he was just that same kind boy from my childhood memory. While the music filled the room, again I felt like I wanted to stay there listening to him play forever. But then he stopped, and the feeling faded away along with the final notes.

Without turning around, Cameron said, "What do you think?"

"It was beautiful."

He turned to look at me and, for just a moment, I thought I saw some warmth creep into those cold blue eyes of his.

"Can't they do something for your hand?" I asked, blurting out the question before I could stop myself.

I was worried he might take offense but he just said calmly, "Not a thing. The nerve damage was too extensive."

"Have you ever thought about going to music school?"

"Yes," Cameron said. "I've thought about it. But it wouldn't work. I can't leave this house."

"Why not?"

For a moment he was silent. Then he said, "Last time I left, I came back to find our mother had had a nervous breakdown and been committed to a mental hospital. I haven't seen her since. I won't make that mistake again."

He turned back to the piano and played a few random chords. With his dark head bent over the instrument, his burnt hand buried in his pocket, and his long musician's fingers flying over the keys, I just couldn't imagine Cameron hitting another person with a riding crop, or anything else.

"Did you flog Piper's boyfriend with a riding crop?"

Cameron's hand froze suddenly on the keys. "A riding crop?" His eyes narrowed and, for a long moment, I thought he wasn't going to answer the question. But then he looked at me and said, "Yes, I did. It was an ugly business."

"Why did you do it then?"

Cameron fixed me with his cold stare and I had to force myself not to look away. "Someone had to," he said quietly.

So he wasn't even going to deny it. I realized that I'd been hoping he would. I'd hoped that Piper was making it up or, at the very least, that he had some kind of explanation that would make such a violent act less horrifying.

Cameron had clearly had enough of the conversation because he turned back to the piano without another word and started to play another piece—cold music that darkened all the shadows in the room and made ice crackle inside my head. I turned away and left, feeling strangely unhappy.

That night, I decided not to go to sleep but to sit up instead. Lilias had said that the Frozen Charlotte dolls moved around at night. The previous nights I'd been woken up by strange things. This time I hoped I'd get a head start by staying awake. I kept the lights off so no one would know I wasn't asleep. Then, when everyone else had gone to bed, I took my flashlight and camera and crept into Rebecca's room.

After hearing those whispers through the walls, I didn't want to be anywhere near those horrible, creepy things. I wanted to go home and never look back. But I couldn't do that, not until I had the answers I came for. If the dolls moved, I would catch it on my camera and then I could show Uncle James, or Piper, or Cameron, or e-mail my mom. Then at least there'd be other people who would know something strange was going on here and could help me find out what it was. I wouldn't have to do it all by myself.

Sitting there in the room, alone in the dark, the sound of my own breathing seemed loud in my ears. The curtains at the windows weren't drawn and I could see the outline of the Frozen Charlotte dolls in the moonlight. My hands were actually shaking with dread as I watched those still, white shapes in the locked cabinet.

But as the hours dragged by and there was no sign of movement and no whisper of sound, I began to feel less nervous and more idiotic. Staying awake became a torture and all I wanted was to crawl into my bed. Maybe I really had lost it, sitting here in a dark room, staring at dolls in a cabinet and waiting for them to move. If Jay could see me now, crouched on the floor with my camera and flashlight, he'd probably laugh his head off. I could imagine him doubled over the way he used to be when he found something really funny, taking off his glasses so he could wipe away the tears streaming down his face. It was one of the things I'd loved most about him. He was always so ready to laugh, and he made you laugh with him.

I ran both hands through my hair, wishing this could all just be some stupid practical joke. Wishing that Jay would turn on the lights and yell, "Surprise! You should have seen your face! I can't believe you fell for it!"

I thought about giving up and going to bed, but I really wanted to feel like I was doing *something*. And then, in the dark, someone started to hum. It was the same tune I had first heard the night Jay died, that innocuous little "Fair Charlotte" ballad.

I froze, almost paralyzed with fear. I couldn't tell exactly where the humming was coming from, but I knew it was close, really close, so close, that whoever it was must practically be upon me. If I were to reach out my hand I would probably brush against them in the dark.

My fingers fumbled with my flashlight as I hurried to switch it on, convinced that Rebecca would be there, sitting right in front of me, eyeball to eyeball. But when the beam of light sliced through the room, there was no one there, no one at my side or behind me. In fact, despite shining the flashlight this way and that, I could see no one else in the room at all. But the humming continued, so softly, and yet almost deafening in my ears because it was so close.

Then I became aware of the smell. This awful, putrid, rotting stench, all wrapped up in a sick sweetness that made me think of death and decaying flowers.

And suddenly I realized that the smell was coming from me. And it wasn't just the smell. The humming was coming from me too. *I* was the one humming that hateful tune! The smell was coming from my own breath, my own mouth, a rot and decay that spoke of maggots and the grave, as if it wasn't me humming at all, but someone else, someone long dead.

I dropped the flashlight and staggered to my feet, flailing around in a blind panic as I tried to escape that awful presence clinging to me. I could feel it resisting me all the way. It didn't want to let go and I had to fight hard to rid myself of it.

I felt the moment when it left. I became suddenly lighter and, finally, I managed to stop humming. The awful smell faded away but I could still taste death in my mouth and I gave a dry heave, certain I was going to be sick right there on the spot.

But then I heard the soft tread of footsteps on the floor of the corridor outside. I snatched up my flashlight and hurriedly turned it off. Lilias had already caught me in Rebecca's room after bedtime once, and the last thing I wanted was for another member of the family to discover me there, in the middle of the night, like a lunatic. But then I distinctly heard the creak of a step. Whoever it was, they were going downstairs.

The thought flashed through my mind that it was Rebecca out there on the stairs. Somehow, she had used my voice to hum that dreadful song, and now that I had managed to fight her off, perhaps she was going elsewhere.

I picked up my camera and quickly tiptoed out of Rebecca's room, over to the top of the staircase. I arrived just in time to see a shaft of moonlight spill out into the hall downstairs as the front door opened and then quickly closed as whoever it was slipped outside.

Did ghosts open and close doors? But if it wasn't Rebecca, then who could it be? I remembered the little girl, the one that couldn't have been Lilias, skipping around the dead tree in the garden, and wondered whether the same thing could be happening now. Was I following a shadow of some kind—a memory, a ghost? After all, hadn't Rebecca inexplicably left the house in the middle of the night, gone out of the garden, and wandered along the clifftop to her death?

There was only one way to find out who was out there. Moving as quietly as I could, I put my hand on the banister to feel my way, and went down the stairs after them.

TEN

With muffled face and silent lips,
Five miles at length were passed,
When Charles with few and shivering words,
The silence broke at last.

With my heart in my mouth, I stepped off the final stair and hurried across the hall towards the front door. As my hand clapped down on the door handle, a high-pitched voice to my right said, *"Who goes there?"*

"Quiet, Tom!" I hissed, silently cursing the wretched bird.

I saw the figure the moment I stepped outside, their dark silhouette hurrying towards the gate, but they were still too far away for me to make out who they were. As I went down the path after them, the cold wind blowing in from the sea made me shiver. Summer seemed to be so much colder in Skye, and I could taste salt in the sea air.

The garden gate opened and closed and the figure disappeared from view. I quickened my pace down the unfamiliar path, the gravel crunching loudly under my feet. I still hadn't turned on my flashlight, for fear of being seen.

When I reached the gate it was still unlocked, and I threw it open, afraid I would already be too late to see which way the figure had gone. So I was unprepared when a bright light suddenly shone in my eyes and two people screamed in my face.

I screamed back and threw up my arms, but then Piper said, "God, Sophie, you frightened us half to death! We thought you were Cameron!"

I slowly lowered my arms and realized that the bright light came from a moped, the engine still running, and that Piper was standing there with a boy perhaps a year older than us, dressed in jeans and a jacket and carrying a helmet under his arm. He was tall and broad-shouldered with features that would probably be considered handsome—he looked like the kind of boy that all the girls at school would fancy and giggle about, but he had extremely small eyes that seemed to glitter through the dark at me.

"I saw someone leaving the house and I thought it was Lilias," I said, clutching at the first plausible lie I could think of. "So when I saw you open the gate I panicked—"

"Haven't you ever heard of *sleep*?" the boy snapped. "Isn't that what normal people do at this time of night?"

"I don't think they sneak around clifftops on mopeds either, do they?" I replied, irritated by his tone. "I thought it was Lilias going outside and I was worried because of . . . Because of what happened before."

"Are you talking about Rebecca?" the boy said, looking at me with those tiny eyes of his. "I've never heard of anyone freezing to death in July, have you?"

"It's all right," Piper said, laying a hand on the boy's arm. "Sophie knows all about our situation—she won't give us away." She turned to me and said, "Sophie, this is Brett. I'm sorry I didn't tell you we were still seeing each other but, after what happened with Cameron, I'm sure you can understand why."

Now that I knew who he was, I looked at Brett again, but he didn't make a better impression on me the second time around. He was good-looking enough, but there was just something about him that made my skin crawl. Perhaps it was the fact that his eyes were so small, or the slight curl to his lower lip, as if he found himself constantly disgruntled and disgusted by the world, and the people in it.

"Brett and I have to meet in secret now," Piper was saying, "because of Cameron."

"That cripple!" Brett sneered. "If he was anyone else I'd have bashed his head in by now! It's only on account of

Piper that I don't. He's still her brother, after all, even if he is an uptight creep."

"Show Sophie what he did," Piper urged. "She'll understand then."

Brett turned and pulled up his jacket and T-shirt, giving me a clear view of his back. It was covered in angry white marks, a shocking mess of scars that had only recently begun to heal. Piper had told me it was bad, and Cameron hadn't denied it, but I think some part of me still hadn't quite believed it until now.

"Did you . . . Did you report it to the police?" I asked.

Brett pulled down his jacket and turned back around. "Last week," he grunted. "But they said there was nothing they could do because I took so long coming forward."

"That was my fault," Piper said. "I asked him not to make trouble for Cameron."

"I'm not scared of him," Brett insisted, despite the fact that I hadn't suggested he was. "That guy is totally out of his mind, but I'm not scared of him. I could snap him in two if I wanted to. And I'm going to get even with him one of these days. No one takes a crop to me and gets away with it, no matter whose brother they are."

"It doesn't matter now," Piper said, stroking his hand as if soothing a whining dog. "All that matters is that we're together." She glanced at me and said, "You won't say anything, will you? It's easier all around if nobody knows. We're just going to go for a little drive and we'll be back long before anyone misses us."

I glanced at the dark, winding clifftop road, and the trees bending in the wind, and said, "Is that safe?"

"Of course it's safe," Brett said. "I've done it hundreds of times before, haven't I, babe?"

"Brett's a very good driver," Piper agreed.

"But this moped has got learner's plates on it," I said, pointing at them.

"What are you, the police?" Brett said.

"Really, Sophie, it'll be fine," Piper said. "We've done it plenty of times before and nothing's ever happened. Just don't mention it to anyone, okay?"

I nodded reluctantly. "All right."

But I felt deeply uncomfortable as I watched them get on the moped. Brett didn't offer his helmet to Piper, but rammed it onto his own head before swinging his leg over the bike. Piper climbed onto the back and wrapped her arms around his waist, and they took off down the winding road. I watched them go, wishing that I'd never discovered Piper's secret.

For a moment, I felt tempted not to return to the house. To just leave and never look back. But if Rebecca was an evil spirit, if she was dangerous, and if she was here, then it was because of what Jay and I had done. Jay was already dead. Rebecca might go after Lilias next, or

Cameron, or Piper. And I was the only one who was even aware of the danger. So I turned and reluctantly went back through the gate, taking care to lock it behind me.

I went upstairs and ran past Rebecca's room, just like Lilias did. When I climbed into my own bed, I didn't think I would sleep. I was afraid to turn off the light in case I suddenly heard that humming again in the dark, only to find that it was coming from me. Perhaps there was no Rebecca at all. Perhaps it was just me, quietly going crazy and not even realizing it. I'd felt permanently tired since Jay died, and I knew I'd lost weight because my jeans were too big for me now. What if I was actually losing my mind too?

Suddenly, I found myself missing my mom. When I'd looked at her during Jay's funeral I'd been surprised to see that she had tears in her eyes. She'd known him for a long time, like I had, and I knew she had always liked him. On a whim, I grabbed my laptop and sent her an e-mail. It wasn't the cheeriest e-mail I'd ever sent. I didn't say anything about Rebecca or the Frozen Charlottes or spirits, I just told her about how much I was missing Jay. It was a comfort, in a way, to speak about him to someone else who'd known and cared about him.

I felt a little bit better afterwards and managed to sleep, although fitfully, until morning.

The next day I would regret that. Perhaps if I had stayed up all night as I'd originally intended, the disaster that set everything else in motion might never have happened.

I woke up with the sun streaming in through the windows. For a moment I snuggled under the covers, feeling pleasantly drowsy, but then the wind rattled the window frame and I heard the howling that really did sound like voices out on the clifftop. It jerked me properly awake, and I remembered the events of the night before. I hadn't heard Piper come home and the awful thought flashed through my mind that perhaps it was because she hadn't come back at all. Perhaps that idiot boyfriend of hers had driven them both right off the edge of the cliff.

I jumped out of bed, pulled on jeans and a T-shirt, and didn't even bother to brush my hair before rushing from the room, where I managed to collide with Cameron in the corridor. He must have just come from the shower because his hair was still damp and his skin smelled pleasantly of mint.

"Sorry," I gasped, drawing back.

"You're in a hurry this morning," he said, brushing his hair from his eyes. "You must really like your cornflakes, huh?"

I looked up at him, and his blue eyes seemed less cold than they had before. In fact, they seemed almost friendly looking, and for a second there was a hint of laughter there that reminded me a little bit of Jay.

"No, I just . . . Have you seen Piper this morning?" I asked.

"I haven't had that pleasure, no," Cameron replied, raising an eyebrow slightly. "Why?'

"I . . . I need to talk to her about something."

"She's probably downstairs getting breakfast—" Cameron started, but was cut off by the scream.

It sounded like Piper, and it was coming from downstairs.

Cameron and I turned and ran down together, and all the while Dark Tom kept shrieking, over and over again, *"Murder! Murder! Murder!"*

We reached the front entrance just as Piper came running out of the old school hall. Her eyes filled with tears when she saw us. "Oh, Cameron," she said. "Don't go in there. I don't want you to see it—please, please don't go in!"

But he was already striding towards the door and, although she tried to stop him from entering the room, he pushed past her roughly.

I hurried in after him and gasped.

Broken keys, cut strings, splinters of glossy wood.

Someone had done their very best to destroy Cameron's piano.

Many of the keys had been pried loose and lay broken on the floor. The wires had all been slashed through and curled up forlornly from the ruins of the instrument. They had poured water inside it too, and the steady drip-drip as it fell to the stage was the only sound in the room.

"No," Cameron said, so quietly that I wouldn't have heard him if I hadn't been right next to him.

He reached out to grip the back of a nearby couch and I saw that his knuckles had gone completely white.

Behind us, Piper started to cry softly and, out in the lobby, Dark Tom was still shrieking incessantly, *"Murder! Murder! Murder!"*

All the noise soon brought Uncle James, who seemed almost as upset as Cameron. "How could this have happened?" he asked, over and over again. "Didn't anyone hear anything?"

But none of us had heard a thing.

Uncle James called the police, and we checked the house, but nothing else had been disturbed or stolen. It seemed that whoever had done this had been interested only in Cameron's piano and nothing else. "Irreplaceable." Cameron muttered the word under his breath. "It's irreplaceable."

His right hand remained buried in his pocket as always, but I could see that his left was shaking.

"Can you think of anyone with a grudge against you?" one of the police officers asked Cameron when they arrived.

He looked directly at Piper and said flatly, "Brett Taylor."

Piper instantly burst into tears and said, "He was here. Last night, he was here! We went for a drive on his moped but then he dropped me back home and he drove away. He drove away—it couldn't have been him, it just couldn't! Brett would never do a thing like this! I know he wouldn't!"

After what she'd said last night, I was surprised to hear Piper confess about seeing Brett, but I was glad that she had.

"Whether Brett was responsible for the piano or not, how dare you sneak out of this house in the middle of the night?" Uncle James demanded. "Opening that gate after dark is absolutely forbidden, Piper! You know that!"

Piper babbled on with apologies, while her parrot out in the hall kept screaming about murder, and all the time, Cameron just stood and stared at her, a flat look of pure loathing that was almost painful to see. I'd never seen anyone look at another person like that before. He was looking at her as if he wanted to kill her.

When the police finally left, with promises to question Brett, Uncle James called a specialist from town to come and look at the piano. We sat in silence as we waited for him to arrive, not looking at the instrument or one another. It felt more like waiting for a doctor to come and look at a dying patient than a man coming to look at a damaged piano.

The moment he saw the piano he sighed and shook his head. "I'm afraid it's no good," he said. "It's completely beyond repair."

Cameron walked out of the room without a word to anyone, leaving behind him a great silence that seemed to fill up with all the words that none of us were saying.

ELEVEN

Such a dreadful night I never saw,
The reins I scarce can hold.
Fair Charlotte, shivering faintly said,
"I am exceedingly cold."

The police called Uncle James a little later to say that they'd questioned Brett, who'd sworn he had nothing to do with the piano and, since there was no evidence, there was nothing more they could do.

After the piano man had gone, Piper went out to soothe Dark Tom, who was still screaming bloody murder in the hall. The sound of his shrill voice stretched my nerves almost to the breaking point, so I went outside to get away from it.

The wind was still blowing in fiercely from the sea, wild enough to mess up my hair the moment I stepped outside. I wandered down to the garden and found Lilias with her toy ostrich under the burnt tree. I hadn't seen her all morning and I assumed she was just trying to stay out of the way.

"Is Cameron going to be okay?" she asked, staring up at me with huge eyes.

"I hope so," I said. "Perhaps . . . Perhaps your dad will be able to buy him a new piano?"

But Lilias shook her head. "There's no money," she whispered.

I plunked myself down next to her and, for a while, we sat together in silence, listening to the moan of the wind and looking back towards the house.

"I hate those dolls!" Lilias burst out suddenly.

I looked down at her fierce expression and said, "It wasn't the dolls who broke the piano, Lilias. Even if they could move around, they're far too small to do damage like that."

"They might not have broken it but it's still their fault," Lilias said. "I know it. They're always telling people to do bad things." I felt her small body shudder beside me, then she whispered, "Convincing. They're so convincing. They twist everything up inside your head until you're not sure what's right anymore. I don't know how they do it, but somehow they can make it seem like a good idea to do a bad thing. They see right inside your head to where the secret thoughts are. That's why I don't talk to them anymore. I talk to Hannah instead." She hugged the toy ostrich to her chest. "She just wants me to be good. She's my real friend." She looked at me and said, "Do you hear that?"

"I can't hear anything except the wind. And the sea."

Lilias nodded. "It's only the wind and sea here now. The birds don't come near the house but they're everywhere on the clifftop, all the way to Neist Point. We never get any rabbits in the garden. No squirrels. No butterflies. I'm glad the butterflies don't come here anymore," she said, picking at the grass beside her.

Now that she'd mentioned it, the garden did seem oddly quiet. There was no birdsong, no rustle of small animals moving through the bushes, no bright eyes peering down from the branches of the trees.

"Well, Shellycoat seems happy enough in the house," I said, trying to find some logical objection to what she was saying.

"She never goes upstairs," Lilias said. "Never. She doesn't mind being downstairs, but if you try to take her upstairs she goes crazy. Cameron tried to take her up there once, when they were putting new carpets in downstairs. She almost scratched his face off. And the yowling. I never heard any cat sound like that before. Cameron said it was like she'd turned into a different cat. He said that something must have spooked her. But I know it was the Frozen Charlottes. They never speak to boys—only girls—so Cameron's never heard them. He just thinks they're creepy dolls."

"What about Dark Tom?" I asked. "Would he go upstairs?"

Lilias considered this for a moment, then shrugged. "Dark Tom is Dark Tom," she said. "Anyway, the butterflies used to make me really sad. The Frozen Charlottes ripped off their wings and left them all around the house. Once I pulled back the covers to get into bed and it was covered in wings."

"What was?" I asked, startled.

"The mattress," she said. "I told Cameron, but he didn't believe me about the dolls. He thought Piper had done it and he got really angry with her." Her voice took on an almost dreamy quality. "They were all different colors. Pretty. So pretty."

The unwelcome image of the vase of flowers in my bedroom came to mind, all fresh and beautiful when I first arrived at the house but shriveled up and dead by the time dinner was over.

"Their faces are inside the tree," Lilias said.

"What?"

"The dolls. Their faces are in the tree." She twisted and pointed at the dead tree behind us.

I looked around to follow her pointing finger and, this time, I saw what I hadn't noticed before. Part of the way up the trunk, just where a few scorched boards still nestled between the burnt branches, were a whole load of faces. You had to know they were there in order to see them, since they were tiny and blackened and blended in with the rest of the tree. But now I could see that there were a dozen or so Frozen Charlotte heads peering down at us from the bark.

"How . . . How did they get there?" I asked, shivering at the sight of them.

"Daddy says they must have melted into the tree during the fire," Lilias said. "There used to be a tree house and Rebecca was playing up there with the dolls when the fire started."

"Was Cameron there too?" I asked.

"No, he saw the fire from the house," Lilias said, "and he ran out to save Rebecca. Don't you think that was brave of him? Daddy says Rebecca probably would have died in the fire if it hadn't been for Cameron. She was stuck up there, you see, and Cameron got her out. That's how he hurt his hand." She looked at me and said, "Do you think it would be better to burn or to freeze to death?"

"I don't know," I said.

"What would you choose if you had a choice between burning to death, freezing to death, or being sliced up with a knife?"

"It doesn't sound like much of a choice," I replied. "I wouldn't like any of them."

"Me neither," Lilias said. "But I think I'd rather burn or freeze than get the knife. I think the knife would hurt the most. Daddy has lots of knives in the kitchen," she went on. "He locked them away because he thinks I might try to cut out my bones, but I'd never do that. I'm stronger than the evil skeleton now." She fingered her collarbone through the fabric of her turtleneck and I felt the sudden urge to take her hand and squeeze it.

"There is no evil skeleton, Lilias," I said gently. "There's only you."

"The Frozen Charlotte dolls killed Rebecca," Lilias whispered, ignoring what I'd said. "They didn't manage it the first time so they had to try again." She glanced up at the tree and said, "It's good that they're up there. They're trapped—they can't get out of the tree." Then she looked at me with those serious eyes of hers and said sadly, "But there's still all the other ones back at the house."

Piper appeared just then, walking across the lawn towards us. She'd wiped her eyes dry but they were still red and blotchy. It was the first time I'd seen her look anything less than perfect.

"Sophie, would you help me with something in the house?" she asked.

"What is it?"

"Just a small thing. Come on, I'll show you."

I left Lilias under the tree and went back to the house with Piper, following her up the stairs to her room. As she shut the door behind us, I noticed the bandage around her right hand.

"What happened to your hand?" I asked.

"Oh. It's silly, really. I fell off Brett's bike last night and twisted it. That's why I need your help, actually."

"You fell off the bike?" I said, alarmed. "Are you all right?"

"Oh yes, I'm fine. But the problem is that I promised to write to my friend, Sally—she's just moved to England, you see. Only now that I've hurt my hand, I can't do it. Would you mind writing the letter for me?"

"Now?"

"If you don't mind."

"Don't you e-mail?"

"Oh no. E-mail is so impersonal. I prefer to write letters. You don't mind, do you? Only she'll worry if she doesn't hear from me."

I thought today of all days was a strange time to be bothering with such things, but I took the pen and paper she gave me and proceeded to write down the words she dictated.

It was a pretty boring letter, mostly about the weather they'd been having, and the different birds Piper had

spotted on her clifftop walks. As I wrote it out for her, I found myself feeling more and more annoyed that she could be bothered with something like this when her brother's priceless piano had just been destroyed, probably by her own boyfriend.

"So, did you actually see Brett drive away?" I asked, handing her the finished letter.

"Gosh, your handwriting is a bit of a mess, isn't it?" Piper said, peering at it with a concerned expression. "I do hope Sally is able to read it."

"Piper, did you see him?" I asked, refusing to be put off.

"Who?" She looked up at me. "Cameron?"

"No, Brett! Did you actually see him drive away from the house?"

"Oh yes, he drove away all right," she said. "I don't believe he was the one who destroyed the piano for a second." She sniffed and said, "But it would serve Cameron right if he had."

I stared at her. "That's a terrible thing to say."

She seemed genuinely surprised. "Is it? You saw the state of Brett's back. Isn't attacking another person far worse than dismantling a piano?"

I supposed she had a point, but I found her behavior a strange contrast to the tears she had shed so copiously earlier.

"I'm devastated for Cameron, of course," she said. "Simply devastated. But I can't say he didn't have it coming. Come on—let's go and make lunch."

Cameron didn't come down for lunch and the rest of us ate around the table in silence. Afterwards I went to the schoolroom and reexamined the photo of Rebecca on the wall. I'd been so intent on her face last time that I hadn't noticed she was holding something. It was a Frozen Charlotte doll.

"Poor Rebecca," Piper said from behind me in a sad voice. I turned and saw her standing in the doorway, fingering her Frozen Charlotte necklace. "Things would have been so different for all of us if she hadn't died."

"Why do you think she left the house in the middle of the night?" I asked.

"I don't know, Sophie. Really, why would anyone go out in the middle of the night when it was dark and howling and there was snow everywhere? She knew she wasn't allowed to. She ought to have been at home in bed." She sighed. "But anyway, I came to ask if you'd like to come camping with us on the beach tomorrow?"

"Us?"

"Me, Brett, and a few other friends. We often go down to the beach during the summer, make a fire, have a barbecue, and sleep outside. It's a ton of fun. You can borrow a sleeping bag."

I thought back to how angry Uncle James had seemed earlier. If my mom or dad had caught me sneaking out like Piper had done, even without the piano incident, I probably would have been grounded for weeks.

"But . . . what about your dad . . ."

"Oh, don't worry about him," Piper said, waving her hand. "I said that we'd already arranged the camping, just for you, and that you're really excited about it and everything. You'll come, right? He might not let me go otherwise. I was going to ask you before, I just never got around to it."

"Won't we get washed away in weather like this?" I asked, glancing out the window at the trees bending in the wind.

"Oh, it's going to die down tomorrow. I checked the forecast." She smiled at me. "I think it would do you good to get out of the house. You look terribly tired, you know, even Dad's noticed it and he never notices anything. I don't think you can be sleeping very well here. A night on the beach, in the fresh air, will probably do you a world of good."

In fact, ever since last night I'd just wanted to go home. After what had taken place in Rebecca's room, and finding out Piper's secret, and then what had happened to Cameron's piano, home seemed so warm and safe and *normal*. But a night spent away from the Frozen Charlottes and this stifling, airless house would be something, at least. "All right," I said. "Thanks."

"Great. We'll head down there around six-ish. Oh, and Sophie, would you mind not mentioning that Brett's going to be there? I sort of skipped over that part with Dad. You know what parents are like."

I couldn't help it—I groaned out loud. "Piper, look, I'm not a snitch but I'd rather not have to lie to your dad."

"You won't have to lie to him," Piper said. "Don't worry, he's not going to start questioning you about it. You just have to keep your mouth shut, that's all. You can do that, can't you? Please, Sophie? As a personal favor?"

I sighed. "All right."

She beamed. "I knew I could count on you."

After she left, I went upstairs and saw that Mom had responded to my e-mail. I wasn't in the mood to reply right then, so I ran a bath instead. But even though the water was hot when I first stepped in, it seemed to cool down really quickly. Frowning, I reached out, trying to turn the tap on for another blast of hot water. But my hand was only halfway there when I gasped—the water in the bath wasn't just cooling down now, it was ice cold. I put my hands on either side of the bath, intending to pull myself out.

The moment I lifted out my hands, the water in the bath started to freeze, actually freeze, around me. Ice blasted across the surface, snapping and crackling as it went—burning me with a ferocious cold that made my skin feel like it was being stripped from my bones in slices, like my body was no longer flesh and blood, but porcelain that would shatter at the slightest touch.

Although my arms were free, I couldn't get out of the bath because the ice had sealed me in completely, the same way the plaster had sealed the Frozen Charlotte dolls into the wall of the basement. When I tried to pull myself up I felt my skin tear and a red swirl ran through the ice, scarlet mixing with white in a way that was disturbingly beautiful.

I opened my mouth and screamed.

Or at least, I tried to.

But I couldn't make a single sound because my throat was suddenly clogged with something, something that threatened to choke me. My chest heaved and I found myself coughing up great clumps of black sand that landed in wet lumps upon the frozen surface of the water.

And then it was over. As quickly as it had started, everything was gone—the ice and the sand, and I was once again lying in a steaming hot bath.

Splashing water everywhere, I scrambled out of the tub and landed in a shivering heap on the bath mat. Even though the water was now warm again, I could still feel that ice against my skin, a cold that pierced all the way through to the bone, and try as I might, I couldn't stop my teeth from chattering, and my skin felt frostbitten and sore.

Finally, I managed to get to my feet, and that was when I saw the words written in the condensation on the mirror:

Charlotte is cold . . .

TWELVE

He cracked his whip,
He urged his steed much faster than before.
And thus five other dreary miles,
In silence were passed over.

Grabbing a towel to wrap around myself, I ran out of the bathroom and down the stairs to find Uncle James. He was sitting at his easel and looked startled when I burst into his studio.

"Sophie," he said, standing up. "What—"

"I can't do this," I said. "I'm sorry, I thought I could, but I can't. I've got to go. I've got to go home right now."

"Home? But . . . But why? What's happened?"

I shook my head, feeling close to tears. I couldn't tell him. He'd never believe me. No one would. I barely believed it myself. "Nothing. I just want to go home."

"All right, we'll talk about it but . . . but would you mind putting some clothes on first?"

"What's going on down here?" Cameron said behind me. I turned and saw him standing in the doorway, staring. "Why are you running around half naked like that?"

"I . . . the bath, it . . . Look, it doesn't matter! All that matters is that I'm going home."

Uncle James was starting to look quite alarmed. "But what would your mother say? I mean, they're not even in the country. I can't just let you go back to an empty house. Whatever the problem is, I'm sure we can sort it out."

I wished I'd paused to put some clothes on. Dripping wet, I was starting to shiver. Cameron must have noticed too because, to my surprise, I suddenly found his jacket draped over my shoulders. I glanced back at him, startled. "Thanks."

He shrugged.

I turned to Uncle James and said, "If you won't drive me back to the ferry, then I'll call a taxi. You can't stop me from going."

Uncle James looked helplessly at Cameron.

"Well, she's right," Cameron said. "We can't keep her here against her will. She's not a prisoner, after all." He looked at me and said, "I'm sure you've got other friends you can stay with at home, right?"

I nodded. "Yes, I'll call someone from the car."

"Well, I really wish you'd reconsider," Uncle James began. "I mean, whatever's upset you—"

"Maybe she just needs to be around friends right now, Dad," Cameron interrupted in a mild tone. "Let's just do as she's asked and take her back to the ferry."

Uncle James ran his hands through his hair. "But I don't know if they'll even be running in weather like this." As if on cue, the windows rattled in their frames as the wind outside shook the house. "There was even talk of closing the bridge this morning."

I could feel sobs of frustration bubbling up inside me and I had to fight hard to shove them back down. "Then I'll stay in a B&B and catch a ferry in the morning," I said. "I *have* to go. I can't stay in this house another minute."

"That's that then," Cameron said. "Call me when you're ready and I'll carry your bags down."

I nodded, thankful for once that Cameron had always been so eager to get rid of me. I went back upstairs before Uncle James could argue with me anymore, got changed as fast as I could, and practically threw my stuff into my bags. When there was a knock at the door I thought it would be Cameron coming for the suitcase, but, in fact, it was Lilias.

"Are you leaving?" she asked.

"Yes," I replied. "I am."

I felt like such an idiot for thinking I could do this in the first place. I wasn't a detective or a ghost hunter. I never should have come.

"She says I have to tell you before you go," Lilias said.

"Who? Tell me what?" I was only half paying attention to her as I finished throwing clothes into my bag.

"Rebecca. She says I have to give you the message."

I stopped what I was doing and looked at her. "What message?"

"She said to tell you that Jay says hello." I felt all the blood drain from my face.

Jay says hello . . .

The words were like a kick in the gut. I felt cold all over, and tears pricked my eyelids. I blinked quickly, trying to force them away, trying to keep myself together. The expression on my face must have worried Lilias because she shrank back from me, as if afraid I was going to smack her or something. She looked terrified all of a sudden.

"I don't want you to go," she said quietly. "And neither does Hannah." Then she turned and ran from the room, almost colliding with Uncle James in the doorway. He was wearing his jacket and had a worried expression on his face. His car keys dangled loosely from his hand.

"Is it because of this business with Cameron's piano?" he asked. "Is that why you want to leave?"

"No." I shook my head. "It's nothing like that. I've just been feeling a bit homesick."

"Well, stay tonight, at least," Uncle James said. "And if you're still feeling homesick in the morning, then I promise I'll take you to the ferry."

Part of me wanted to insist on leaving right now. I so badly wanted to go. But what would happen then? Rebecca would still be here. Lilias would still be afraid. My uncle and cousins would still be in danger. And Jay and I were the ones to blame for all of it. If we'd never messed around with the Ouija-board app, none of this would have happened. Jay was gone. I was the only person left who could try to undo the damage we'd done.

"Please, Sophie," Uncle James said softly. "If you leave upset like this you might regret it by the time you get home."

I knew he was right. I probably would regret it. For the rest of my life.

"All right," I heard myself say. "I'll stay."

I wanted to get out of the house for a while, so I told Uncle James I needed some fresh air and was going for a walk. The wind was still blowing fiercely, so he made me promise not to go too close to the edge of the cliff before he'd let me go.

I didn't get very far before Cameron caught up with me, planting himself on the path in front of me so that I had to stop. I could feel a blush creeping up my cheeks and really wished Cameron hadn't been around for my conversation with Uncle James. He must think I was a total basket case.

"Running around in towels one minute and stomping along clifftops the next," he said, staring at me. "I can hardly keep up with you. Dad says you've changed your mind about leaving. Will you at least tell me what she did?"

For a confused moment, I thought he meant Rebecca. "Who?"

"Piper, of course."

I thought of the water freezing around me in the bath, and the black sand that had clogged my throat, and shook my head. "Piper had nothing to do with it."

"Look, it might seem that way to you but, trust me, whatever it was, whatever happened, Piper was responsible."

"Do you think Piper is a witch?"

Cameron looked confused. The wind blew his hair into his eyes and he brushed it away impatiently. "Of course I don't think she's a witch."

"Then she couldn't have been responsible for what happened earlier. And why are you so hung up on this, anyway? Piper and I have been getting along fine ever since I arrived, so what makes you think she'd go out of her way to be horrible?"

To my surprise, Cameron laughed, an unsteady, sudden laugh that burst out of him without warning.

"Because," he said, "that's her nature. She doesn't need a reason, you didn't have to do anything to her. She sees opportunities for mindless cruelty everywhere, and she takes them. How do you think Lilias got her fear of bones?"

"But . . . But how could Piper possibly be responsible for that?"

Cameron shook his head and stared out towards the gray sea below us. "She's so clever about it nobody ever guesses the truth. When Lilias was a baby, I heard her crying one day. It wasn't her normal cry, not the kind she'd do if she was hungry or tired, this was more of a scream. I was afraid she'd hurt herself somehow so I went running into her room. When I saw Piper standing by the cot I thought she'd gone to comfort her. But then I realized she was pinching her as hard as she could. Pinching her on her arm hard enough to create a great black bruise there. She was just standing by the cot, smiling down at Lilias while she screamed."

The idea sent a chill through me. I hugged my jacket closer and said, "But that doesn't explain why Lilias is afraid of bones."

"When Lilias was about three years old, Piper said she wanted to take her up to bed and read her a story," Cameron replied. "At the time I thought it meant she was warming to Lilias a bit. After Rebecca died, Mom sort of withdrew into herself and wasn't always aware when Lilias needed something, and Dad just shut himself away with his brushes and paints. I watched out for Lilias and I made sure she wasn't left by herself all the time. So when Piper wanted to read to her I was happy—I thought she wanted to help. But then, a few weeks later, I noticed that there'd been a change in Lilias. She was quiet, nervous, subdued, not herself at all. I never thought to connect the change with Piper's bedtime stories, but one day I went upstairs earlier than normal and I heard the story Piper was telling Lilias. She wasn't reading from any book. She'd made up something special for our sister. A ghastly story about how there was an evil skeleton inside her that wanted to take control of her body and do all kinds of awful things. She'd been telling her these stories for weeks. That was when Lilias developed her fear of bones, a fear she hasn't been able to recover from since."

"Perhaps Piper didn't realize how frightening her stories were," I said, not wanting to believe what he was saying.

"She knew," Cameron said. "Piper doesn't do anything by accident. Do you think it was just by chance that Lilias ended up with a bone in her steak the night you arrived? The entire episode was a carefully staged spectacle, specially designed for your benefit and Piper's own grotesque pleasure. The same way it wasn't an accident that she served me food she knew I wouldn't be able to eat without assistance. And, later, when she asked me to play 'Sweet Seraphina' on the piano, she knew perfectly well that I can no longer play that tune. Piper is a master of death by a thousand cuts. How do you think our mom ended up in a mental hospital?"

I shook my head, not quite knowing what to say. "I told you I went away—I made the mistake of going to a music summer school one year, and when I got back I found that Mom had been committed while I was gone. She said she kept hearing Rebecca's voice calling out to her when no one else was around. Piper is an excellent mimic. She'd deny it, of course, but I'd bet my life that she put on Rebecca's voice, just for the sake of tormenting Mom. There was an incident with some pills . . . Mom was lucky to survive. She might have been okay in the end, if Piper could have just left her alone. That's why it's not safe for you here. That's why I still think you should go."

I was trembling from head to feet, hardly able to take in what Cameron was saying. "I can't," I whispered.

"Why not, for God's sake?"

"Because of Rebecca."

He stared at me. "Rebecca? What can she possibly have to do with any of this? She's dead."

"I came here to find out how she died."

Cameron shook his head impatiently and turned away from me. "I don't want to talk about Rebecca."

"I know you blame her for what happened to your hand," I said. "And for starting that fire."

Cameron slowly turned around to face me, and the look on his face was so frightening that it took all of my willpower not to take a step back from him.

"Rebecca didn't start the fire," he said. "Piper did."

THIRTEEN

Said Charles, "How fast the shivering ice,
Is gathering on my brow."
And Charlotte, still more faintly said,
"I'm growing warmer now."

P iper started the fire?" I said. "But I thought Rebecca was in the tree house when it happened?"

"She was. She was up there playing when the fire started. I saw the smoke from my bedroom window. And you know what else I saw? Piper standing on the grass staring up at the tree house as smoke poured out of it and flames blackened the leaves and Rebecca called and called for help. But Piper just stood and watched and smiled and did nothing."

"What are you saying?" I asked, horrified. "That Piper actually wanted Rebecca to . . . to *die* in the fire?"

Cameron took a deep breath and exhaled hard through his nose. "Of course not," he said quietly. "I didn't say that, and I'm not suggesting it. All I'm saying is that Piper is not a good person for you to be around and that you shouldn't stay here. You should leave—you should get off this island and never look back."

"I'm not leaving."

"Must I beg you to go?" Cameron snapped. "Do you want me on my knees, is that it? Do you really want to end up like Lilias and me?" He took his burnt hand out of his pocket and held it up in plain sight, but this time I refused to flinch. "*This* is what will happen if you don't leave. Sooner or later, there'll be some accident, some unforeseen incident, something will happen . . . and you'll get hurt." He shoved his hand back into his pocket. "Do you want to leave here with more scars than you came with?"

"My best friend died," I said, finally managing to say the word. "Before I came here."

Cameron frowned. "Yes, I know," he said. "And I'm sorry. But I don't see what that—"

"We were at this café, messing around with a Ouija-board app on his phone," I said. "When Jay asked me who we should speak to, I said Rebecca—her name just popped into my head. And then the board confirmed it was her. I *know* it sounds ridiculous, but you weren't there. Something terrible happened that night. All the lights in the café went out, everyone started screaming, one of the waitresses was horribly burnt. And Jay died. I think we spoke to Rebecca and she got out of the board and now I've brought her back here to the house with me. She's angry and she wants something, but I don't know what it is."

Cameron stared at me, and a long moment stretched taut between us. The waves hammered the rocks, the wind battered the cliffs, and seagulls screamed at each other in the distance.

Finally, he said, "What do you expect me to say to that? Do you actually believe it or are you as unhinged as everyone else around here?"

"It's the truth."

He threw up his hands. "All right, so it's the truth! So what? If this Jay truly was your friend then he wouldn't want you in harm's way, would he? If he were here, then he'd tell you to go home."

"You don't get to speak for him!"

"Look, I know I never met him, that I don't know the first thing about him, but I'm telling you that if he was any kind of friend to you at all, then he wouldn't want you here with us."

I knew that Cameron was right. I could almost hear Jay's voice inside my head, not joking like it normally was, but quiet and serious instead. *Go home, Sophie. Please.*

But we were the ones who had let Rebecca out. And I was the one who'd brought her back to Skye. She could hurt Lilias next, or Cameron, or Piper, and it would be my fault. What if I went home and then a few weeks later we received a telephone call from Uncle James to say that Lilias had frozen to death in the bathtub? Or that Piper had fallen down the stairs and broken her neck?

"Rebecca is here," I said. "I know she is. I've felt her."

I wanted to tell Cameron about the Frozen Charlotte dolls scratching at the glass, the music box playing in the middle of the night, the little girl skipping around the burnt tree, the cold fingers curling around mine, the strange experience in Rebecca's bedroom with the humming and the rotten smell of death and, finally, the way the bath had turned to ice around me and the writing that had appeared on the mirror. But the expression on his face made me falter. How could I ever expect him to believe me?

"I've felt her," I repeated feebly. "And Lilias has seen her. She's spoken to her too."

A dark look came over Cameron's face at the mention of Lilias's name, and in a couple of strides he had covered the distance between us. His left arm reached out towards me and I thought he was going to grab me, but then, at the last moment, he clenched his fingers into a fist and dropped his hand to his side instead.

"I don't know if you're actually demented, or as big a liar as Piper, or if you're just grieving for your friend, and to be honest I don't really care, but if you breathe one word of this nonsense to Lilias, I'll—"

"You'll what?" I demanded. I knew all this was a lot for anyone to accept but I refused to be bullied, not by Cameron or anyone else. With both hands I shoved him back so hard that he stumbled over his feet and almost ended up on the ground. "Flog me with a riding crop like you did to Brett?"

Cameron clamped his jaw shut and I distinctly saw a muscle twitch there. "Say whatever you like to me," he said quietly. "Repeat this fantasy to Piper and my dad if you must, but don't bring Lilias into it. She's terrified of Rebecca's room and lives in a state of constant fear as it is without you convincing her that our dead sister is haunting the house as well. I won't have life made any more difficult for her than it already is."

"I know you don't believe me," I said, "and I can't really blame you for that, but Rebecca *is* here—I'm sure of it. And I think she might be dangerous."

Cameron was silent for a moment. Finally, he said, "This was a mistake. I realize that now. You clearly need some time to yourself to calm down."

I watched as, silently fuming, he turned and walked away.

Dinner that night was a strained event, which wasn't much of a surprise considering what had happened with Cameron's piano that morning and the drama I'd managed to cause in the afternoon. I noticed that Uncle James kept shooting nervous glances at me, as if he half thought I might stand up and demand to leave again at any moment. At the end of the meal he cleared his throat and said, "I'm taking Lilias into town tomorrow for her therapy session. I spoke to her therapist on the phone earlier and she said that if you'd like to have a word with her too then she could see you for half an hour after Lilias has finished."

It took me a moment to realize that Uncle James was looking at me. "Why would I want to talk to a therapist?" I asked. I glared across the table at Cameron, thinking he must have told his dad about the conversation we'd had earlier, but then Piper said, "Oh, I hope you don't mind, Sophie, but I told Dad about how you've been . . . well . . . struggling since Jay died." She smiled at me, absently playing with the Frozen Charlotte necklace at her throat, her fingers stroking the doll's white porcelain cheek.

My face felt suddenly hot. Everyone was looking at me. "Struggling?" I said. "Well, I lost someone and I miss him, but I wouldn't call that struggling. That's just normal, isn't it?"

"Of course," Uncle James said at once. "Of course. Perfectly normal. It was only a thought, that's all. But if you don't want to go then there's an end to the matter."

When we went upstairs to bed I stopped Piper in the corridor outside our rooms and said, "Why did you say those things to your dad?"

She looked genuinely surprised. "You don't mind, do you? I just thought it might help you to talk to someone, that's all. I know a lot of people don't like the idea of therapists, but this one is really good. She's helped Lilias a lot. I've heard that grief counseling can be really helpful for some people. I hope you don't think I betrayed your confidence by speaking to Dad. I'd be mortified if you thought that, really I would."

I stared at her for a moment in silence. She seemed so completely genuine, and there was a look of real concern in her eyes as she gazed at me.

"You're not cross with me, are you?" Piper asked, putting a hand on my arm. I noticed she no longer had a bandage on it, which seemed strange. In fact, there didn't seem to be anything wrong with her hand at all. "I'm so sorry if I did the wrong thing."

"Never mind," I said. "Just forget it."

She went to her room and I was glad to see her go. I went to my room and had only been there a minute or so when there was a soft tap at my door. I opened it to find Lilias on the other side. She glanced up and down the corridor, as if afraid of being overheard, then she leaned closer to me and said, "Be careful tonight. One of them got out."

"One of them?" I frowned. "Are you talking about the Frozen Charlotte dolls?"

Lilias nodded. "I counted them," she said. "Just now. One of them is missing. One of them got out. You should check your room. Make sure it's not in here and then lock your door. Don't open it till the morning."

"But Lilias—"

"I don't want to go blind, do you? Lock your door if you don't want to end up like that girl in the photo."

"All right, but what about the others?"

"Others?"

"Cameron and Piper."

"The dolls wouldn't hurt Piper," Lilias said, as if that were obvious. "And Cameron doesn't believe in them so I'm going to tell him the evil skeleton is speaking to me again. That way he'll sleep on the chair in my room all night and I can keep him safe. The dolls want to hurt Cameron most of all."

"Why Cameron most of all?"

"Because Piper hates him." Lilias curled her lip in contempt. "He's the best brother in the whole world ever but Piper hates him because he can really see her." Her hands clenched into fists at her side, and she went on. "Sometimes I have nightmares that the dolls get to him and they poke his eyes out with their needles and then he's blind and he can't play the piano anymore and that would make him so sad, sadder than anything else in the world. But I'm never ever going to let that happen. Not to Cameron. I'll stamp on all their ugly little rotten heads if they ever come near him."

After Lilias disappeared down the hall to her own room, I closed my door, hesitated a moment, and then locked it. I checked the room and couldn't see any Frozen Charlotte dolls around.

All Lilias's talk about going blind made me think of the black-and-white photo downstairs in the old classroom, of the schoolmistress who used to live in the house, standing outside with all of her pupils, including the girl with the blindfold. Suddenly, something I'd heard the Frozen Charlottes whisper came floating back to me:

Let's play the Push-Teacher-Down-the-Stairs Game!

I could see the teacher's stern, serious face in the photo and my hands turned clammy as I pictured that steep flight of stairs outside my door and the thought that had gone through my mind when I first saw them: *stairs to break your neck on* . . .

I wiped my hands on my jeans. It couldn't be true. When the school closed down, the teacher probably just moved on to teach at some other school in the village. Or perhaps she got married and moved away with her husband, somewhere far away from Skye and the schoolhouse and the Frozen Charlottes locked up in the basement.

I shook my head, trying to clear it of the image of the teacher lying at the foot of the stairs with her neck broken. But I couldn't get the thought out of my head and knew I wouldn't be able to until I'd proved to myself that it hadn't happened like that. So I turned my laptop on and googled the old schoolhouse on the clifftop.

I instantly wished that I hadn't.

The school's last teacher had not, as I had hoped, moved away when the school shut down, or gone to teach at another school. She was the reason the school closed in the first place. The local newspaper had covered it all in an article, printed alongside the same class photo I'd seen downstairs.

Although a thriving school for many years, the Dunvegan School for Girls was dogged by misfortune towards the end of its tenure, culminating in the death of schoolmistress, Miss Grayson, when she fell down the stairs and broke her neck. Although advertisements went out for a replacement teacher, it seems the school's troubled reputation put off potential applicants and, as a result, the decision was eventually made to close the school.

In the final years before the school closed for good, one of the students died in a bizarre accident involving an overlooked allergy, while another came into difficulty swimming in nearby Loch Pooltiel and drowned. A further accident left a student permanently blind in both eyes, and another girl fell to her death from one of the upstairs windows.

Today, the house is occupied as a private residence by the Craig family, but it seems its curse is alive and well. Cameron Craig, a child prodigy whose rising star looked set to shine bright in the music world, had his promising career cut short when a fire on the grounds caused irreparable damage to one of his hands. A short while later, his younger sister, seven-year-old Rebecca Craig, froze to death one night on the clifftop under mysterious circumstances . . .

Burnt, frozen, drowned, poisoned, maimed, and killed . . . there seemed to be no end to the horrors that had occurred in the house or the area around it. The building had been a school since the 1850s but the first sign of anything strange going on seemed to be around 1910. What had changed? Could it be something to do with the Frozen Charlotte dolls? Perhaps they'd come into the house at around that time?

I was just trying to think how I could find out more about the Frozen Charlottes when the discordant peal of piano keys rang out from downstairs. It was almost 3 a.m., and I jumped at the sudden sound in the silent house.

I relaxed a moment later when I realized it must just be Shellycoat walking across the keys again like she had the night I arrived. I went back to looking at the article on my laptop, but then the clash of keys came again and, this time, shock surged through me as I remembered.

There was no piano downstairs anymore.

FOURTEEN

So on they rode through frosty air,
And glittering cold starlight.
Until at last the village lamps,
And the ballroom came in sight.

The crash and groan of tuneless notes continued, growing ever more frantic, as if a demented halfwit sat down there, pounding mindlessly at the keys in some kind of lunatic frenzy.

I snatched my camera from the bed and ran down the stairs before I could lose my nerve. I was sure the rest of the family would be close behind me because the music was pretty loud by now—a terrible din that was sure to wake the entire house.

I hesitated for a moment outside the old school hall before throwing open the door and stepping inside.

The huge room was dark, but the moonlight shining in through the windows behind the stage clearly illuminated the piano as a dark silhouette. I'd seen the piano man take the ruined instrument away with my own eyes and yet here it was, perfectly whole once again.

And that wasn't all. Someone was hammering away at the piano keys, the silhouette clear in the moonlight.

It was a little girl wearing a dress, long hair trailing down her back. She was pounding at the keys like she hated the instrument with all her soul, and hated the music even more.

She slammed her fingers down a few more times with jerky, unnatural movements, as if she was a puppet on strings, yanked around by a puppet master with no skill. Even from across the room I could sense her mounting frustration and anger, as if she was trying to play a tune she couldn't remember the music to.

And then, all of a sudden, it shifted slightly, and even though the notes were still all wrong and grossly out of tune, I could hear a wobbling melody faintly beneath it. It was a song I knew well and hated—the "Fair Charlotte" ballad.

The girl's hair fell down on either side of her face as she bent her head over the piano and proceeded to murder the folk song so that it was almost unrecognizable.

With fumbling hands, I turned on my camera, lifted it up, and snapped a photo.

The brightness of the flash lit up the room for a brief

second and in that awful moment I clearly saw a girl in a plain white nightgown, long, dark hair trailing over her shoulders and hiding her face from view, seated at a piano that didn't exist anymore, her hands slipping and sliding over the keys because they were so smeared and sticky with blood.

In the last fraction of a second before the flash went dark, Rebecca jerked her face towards me. I saw bloody tears, angry dark circles beneath her eyes, and blue, frozen lips . . .

And then the flash went off, plunging the room into darkness.

I felt a sudden rush of air from the other side of the room, as if a window had just been opened and a current was racing towards me, but I knew this was no mere air current.

I heard things being knocked over and falling to the ground as whatever it was flew closer and closer, and as I stumbled back in the dark, I knew it was almost upon me.

The next moment I felt cold hands, one on each shoulder, and an awful, unbearable heat, the crackle of flames, and the smell of burning. I staggered back and tripped over something on the floor. Long hair brushed against my arm as I fell and then the hem of a damp nightgown swept against my cheek.

By the time I scrambled to my feet and found the light switch in the dark, she'd gone. There was no piano up on the stage, and aside from a knocked-over table and a couple of fallen books, there was no sign that anything had ever been there in the room with me at all.

I snatched up my camera from where it had fallen, praying that I'd managed to capture Rebecca on film. I pressed the button to view my photos, dreading that I would have just captured an empty hall.

But the second the image came up to fill the screen, I felt my heart speed up in my chest, thumping so hard against my ribs that it hurt.

The photo clearly showed a piano up on the stage, and a little girl sitting at it, her head bent over the keys, her long, dark hair veiling her face.

But that wasn't the only thing. Even though the stage was now empty, in the photo it was full of Frozen Charlotte dolls, row upon row of them, covering the entire stage in a sea of white porcelain and curly dark heads. They swarmed up and around the piano, only leaving enough room for the legs. Every doll, big and small, had its face turned towards me, so I could clearly see that their eyes were open and their lips were pinched in cold disapproval. Their raised arms, bent at the elbow, meant that they all had their tiny hands stretched out towards me, and every single one of them had blood on their fingertips, running in delicate streaks down their white palms.

The dolls and Rebecca and the piano made me feel queasy but, in spite of that, I was fiercely pleased that I had managed to photograph her. I went back upstairs and uploaded my new photos to my laptop.

Blown up on the larger screen, the picture showed Rebecca and her dolls even more clearly. After saving the image, I suddenly remembered that I'd never gotten around to looking at the photos I'd taken of Neist Point and the house the morning after I arrived. I clicked to the start and quickly went through the photos of birds I'd taken down at the lighthouse. But then I got to the one I'd taken of the house from the outside, and I froze.

Every single window was white and at first I thought that all the curtains were drawn, but I was sure the windows hadn't been covered when Piper and I returned from our walk. In fact, I didn't think there were any curtains downstairs—that was what made the dark windows so unnerving at night.

But when I zoomed into one of the windows a bit closer, my breath caught in my throat as I realized that the white in the windows wasn't curtains at all—it was hundreds of tiny hands. Small white fingers splayed across the glass, pressing up against the outside world, and I knew at once who they belonged to.

By the time I turned off my computer, it was past 4 a.m. and the dawn light was shining through the windows. My eyes burned and itched with tiredness, so I leaned my head back against the wall, thinking I'd close my eyes for just a few minutes. But I fell straight asleep and woke up a few hours later, feeling stiff, cold, and almost more tired than I had been before I went to sleep.

The rest of the house was still in bed, but I decided to get up anyway. An idea had occurred to me as I drifted off last night and I wanted to act on it as soon as possible. I quickly changed my clothes, pulled a brush through my hair, winced at the sight of my bloodshot eyes staring back at me in the mirror, then went downstairs to the old classroom. I went straight to the black-and-white photo on the wall of Miss Grayson and her students standing outside the school. The article I'd read hadn't mentioned the names of the girls who'd been hurt at the school, but I remembered seeing names neatly printed along the bottom of the photo. It didn't take me long to find the one I was looking for. The name of the girl who'd been blinded was Martha Jones.

Of all the girls, she was the only one whose accident hadn't been fatal, and I was clinging to the hope that she might have gone on to have children, children who might still be alive and living here in Skye and could tell me more about her. I tiptoed back up the stairs to my room, turned on my laptop, and did a search for her. I found out she had lived in the area all her life, in the flat above her family's gift shop, Salty's Gifts. She'd died fifteen years ago, but perhaps someone from the family was still running the business and might know something about what had happened at the school all those years ago. I knew it was a long shot but it was the only thing I could think of. I grabbed my backpack and went back downstairs, where I left a note on the dining room table saying that I was going into town to take some photos of Dunvegan in the morning light and that I'd be back soon.

I was careful to sneak out without any of the family hearing me. I had to be alone for this; the last thing I wanted was Piper deciding she was going to tag along. So I could have throttled Dark Tom when he started squawking the moment I stepped into the front hall.

"*Thief!*" he shrieked, bobbing up and down on his perch. "*Thief! Thief! Thief!*"

"For God's sake, shut up!" I hissed, wondering if it would be really awful of me to reach through the bars and poke him with something sharp. But then I remembered the sugar mice I'd stuffed in my bag to eat on the way, and quickly reached in for one of them, snapped off its head, and pushed it through the bars, hoping that parrots liked sugar.

Thankfully, Dark Tom snatched the treat from me and began pecking at it, leaving me free to slip through the front door and head straight for the bus stop.

There weren't many people around when I arrived in town. It was such a small, sleepy place that I'd hoped to be able to find the gift shop easily, but although I walked around the handful of shops twice, I could see no sign of one called Salty's Gifts.

Finally, I stopped a woman who was passing by and asked her.

"Oh, Salty's closed down years ago. It's The Searock Café now. That one over there."

She pointed across the road. It was small but cheerful looking, with neat little round tables covered with checkered tablecloths.

I walked over to the café just as a group of men who looked like they'd come in from the fishing boats headed out.

As I entered, the little bell above the door announced my presence, and a gray-haired woman who was clearing a table gave me a smile and told me to take a seat. I must have looked a bit deflated because she came bustling over a moment later and said, "You look like you need something to cheer you up. How about a nice hot breakfast?"

She was smiling down at me in such a kindly way and it felt so good to be somewhere normal without ghosts or dolls or other horrors. So I ordered some tea and a bacon roll, and when she brought them to me a few minutes later, the roll tasted every bit as good as it smelled. I could feel myself cheering up a little with each hot, delicious mouthful.

"Well, you certainly seemed to enjoy that," the woman said when she came back to collect my empty plate. "I don't think I've ever seen a teenager up and about this early in the summer before."

"I was hoping to go to Salty's Gift Shop," I said. "But then someone told me it had turned into this café."

"Oh, yes. Salty's closed years ago," the woman said. "Not enough trade in the winter months, unfortunately. Whereas a café gets business even after the tourists have gone. The fishermen alone would keep us going. They build up such a hunger when they're out on the loch. But if it's gifts you're after then there's a little shop a couple of doors down that sells sweets and postcards and things."

I shook my head. "No, I was really hoping to speak with a member of the Jones family."

"Really? Well, I'm Pat Jones. The business still belongs to my family even though it's a café now."

"Oh." Somehow it hadn't occurred to me that the

same family would still be running the place. "Are you related to Martha Jones?"

At the mention of the name, Pat's smile faltered and when she spoke, her voice had lost some of its cheerfulness. "She was my aunt."

"Then perhaps you can help me."

"Is this about what happened at the schoolhouse?" Her voice had definitely grown colder now.

"Yes, I just—"

"I'm sorry but I'm afraid I can't help. It all happened so long ago and I really don't have time to satisfy any morbid curiosity about it."

"It's not morbid curiosity," I said. "Honestly, it isn't like that. I'm staying at the schoolhouse at the moment. The Craigs are family of mine. They live there."

"Oh." She shot me an anxious look.

"I won't take up too much of your time," I said. "Please. I only want to find out how Martha went blind and what happened at the school."

Pat hesitated a moment, and if a customer had walked in just then I'm sure she would have used them as an excuse not to talk to me. But she seemed to make up her mind and pulled out the chair across from me.

"My dear, I really don't know much about it," she said. "It was before my time. I've never even been to the school."

"But did your aunt ever talk about what happened?"

Pat sighed and said, "The truth is that us kids were all rather afraid of her. And she wasn't exactly the type to make friends with children. She used to just sit in the corner, rigid as a board, and stare straight ahead of her, as if she was trying to see with those blind eyes of hers."

"How did she go blind?"

"It was an accident," Pat said, looking down and rubbing at a nonexistent stain on the tablecloth.

"What kind of accident?" I asked.

"We don't really know. She was asleep when it happened."

"Asleep?"

"Yes, she woke up screaming in the middle of the night. Apparently some sewing needles had gotten tangled in her pillow and they said she must have rolled onto them in her sleep. But Aunt Martha always said that . . . well, that someone did it to her. There was a terrible scandal about it at the time and the school was on the brink of being closed anyway when the schoolteacher fell down the stairs. Everyone blamed the teacher, you see, for what was happening to the girls. All those accidents, and she was the one who was supposed to be looking after them."

"I suppose if she was the last person who died then people might have thought that the deaths ended with her because she was the one responsible."

Pat gave me a startled look. "She wasn't the last one to die."

"She wasn't?"

"No. The little girl who jumped from the window died just an hour or so later."

"*Jumped?*" I stared at her. "But I thought she fell?"

Pat flushed and her hands reached out to fiddle with the salt shaker. "Look, this is why I didn't want to get into it," she said. "The families of all those girls still live on the island. The old schoolhouse is a painful subject for those of us who had relatives there at the time. I don't want all of this to get dragged up again. I only know what my aunt told me and you have to understand that she'd been through a dreadful ordeal, going blind like that. Sometimes I think it turned her a little mad."

"I just want to hear her side of it," I said. "You probably know that my uncle and cousins have had a lot of accidents at that house, and Rebecca died on the clifftop."

"It's just bad luck," Pat said, her tone almost pleading. "It doesn't mean anything. There's no such thing as haunted houses."

"Well, what harm would it do to tell me about it, then?"

She sighed. "Aunt Martha blamed the other girls."

"The girls?"

"She said that they turned on one another. At the start of the year they were all friendly and well behaved—good students, you know—and then something changed and some of the girls started misbehaving. Just little things at first, but then it got worse and worse. Aunt Martha believed that the deaths at the school, including Miss Grayson's, weren't accidents. She used to say that it's easier than you think to push someone down the stairs."

"So if they were all well-behaved girls to begin with, what changed?"

Pat shrugged unhappily, and I glanced at the door, worried that a customer would walk in. There wasn't time to tiptoe around the real question, so I just came out with it. "Did it have anything to do with the Frozen Charlotte dolls?"

The quick look she gave told me that she already knew about them. "Are they still there at the house?" she asked.

"Yes. My cousin Rebecca found them in the basement. They'd been plastered into the walls but my uncle chipped them out for her."

"Someone, I don't know who, gave them to the school for the girls to play with. For some reason my aunt developed a kind of phobia about them. It seems that a few of the other girls told her that they could hear the dolls whispering at night and moving around in the toy room. There was some unpleasantness when the school cat got locked in there one night and the next morning it was dead. Aunt Martha said that whenever anything around the place went missing or got broken, the girls would blame it on the Frozen Charlottes. She said that the dolls made the girls evil. But I'm sure it was simply a case of naughty children trying to blame their behavior on toys."

"So you don't think the Frozen Charlotte dolls are dangerous?"

"Of course not. They're only dolls. But . . . Well, I feel quite embarrassed saying this, but I would never have one of them in the house." She shook her head. "It's so silly, but the way my aunt talked about those dolls has stayed with me my entire life. I've never seen one, except in pictures, but if either of my girls had ever brought one home I would have taken it away and gotten rid of it. Maybe your uncle should think about doing the same?"

"And the girl who jumped from the window?" I asked. "Do you think she did it because the dolls told her to?"

"No," Pat replied. "At least . . . my aunt always believed that she did it because she knew she couldn't resist the dolls and so she killed herself so that she wouldn't be able to hurt anyone else. Like I said, it happened the same day the teacher died, so my aunt always believed that this girl pushed their teacher down the stairs and then killed herself."

The bell over the door rang as a family came in, and although Pat gave me a smile, I could tell she was glad to get away from me. So I paid for my breakfast and walked back to the bus stop.

FIFTEEN

They reached the door and Charles sprang out,
He reached his hand for her.
She sat there like a monument,
That has no power to stir.

Piper was waiting for me when I got back to the house, swooping down on me almost the second I walked through the door.

"You should have told me you were going out," she said. "I would have come with you."

"It was a spur-of-the-moment thing. I couldn't sleep so I thought I might as well get up."

"Oh yes, the photos." Piper smiled at me. "Can I see them?"

"There's something wrong with my camera," I said, pleased that my voice came out pretty normal. I was obviously getting good at brazenly lying to people. "I wasn't able to take any."

"What a shame," Piper replied.

We looked at each other for a moment and I sensed that she didn't believe me.

Even though I'd been desperate to show someone my photo of Rebecca, part of me was glad to have a reason not to confide in Piper. Lately, I found myself unsure around her. But that morning, at the first opportunity, I showed the photo to Cameron.

I saw him leave the house from my window later that morning and ran down the clifftop path after him. It was the perfect opportunity since we couldn't be seen or heard that far away from the house. We hadn't really spoken since that awkward conversation on the clifftop the day before, when he'd practically accused me of being a nutcase.

"Cameron," I called, and he stopped and turned back towards me. "I want to show you something."

When I switched on my camera and brought up the saved photos, I was afraid that the one of Rebecca might have mysteriously vanished, but it was still there, just as disturbing as ever.

"Take a look at this," I said, holding it out to him.

Cameron took the camera from me without a word and looked down at the screen. He stared at the picture for a long time before finally looking up.

"Very impressive," he said in an icy voice. "Looks like the kind of thing that would win you first place in any photography competition. Although, I have to say, I'm not sure it's in very good taste."

"This isn't for any competition, you idiot!" I said, losing patience. "This is a photo that I took downstairs in the middle of the night."

"Which night?"

"Last night."

"Impossible. The piano is still there."

"I know! But it happened. Rebecca is here—she's right here in the house with us—and she's trying to tell me something. Something to do with the Frozen Charlotte dolls. I think maybe they had something to do with her death."

"I don't see how," Cameron said, and I could hear the contempt in his voice as he handed the camera back to me. "They're dolls, for God's sake."

He turned and started to walk away, but I hurried after him and grabbed his arm. "You've got to believe me," I said, hating how desperate I sounded. "If even a photograph won't convince you that Rebecca is back, then what will?"

Cameron gazed at me for a moment, then he said, "I'd have to see her with my own eyes. And, even then, I probably wouldn't believe it."

He pulled his arm free and carried on walking, and this time I let him go.

I was standing there, digging my nails into my palms and trying to control the frustration bubbling up inside me, when I felt my phone vibrate in my pocket. I took it out and saw that it was Mom calling. I frowned as I remembered that I hadn't replied to her e-mail. There was a massive time difference between us—it must be the middle of the night in San Francisco.

I pressed the button to answer the call. "Hello?"

"Sophie!" Mom's voice sounded very far away on the other end of the phone, and the wind on the clifftop didn't help.

I pressed the phone closer to my ear. "Mom, I can't hear you very well. Is something wrong?"

"I just wanted to make sure you were okay," Mom said.

"Of course I'm okay," I said. "Look, I'm sorry I didn't reply to your e-mail, but—"

"It's just that you sounded so upset last night."

"What?" I frowned again. "I didn't speak to you last night. Do you mean the e-mail?"

". . . can't hear you very well, Sophie," Mom said. I could just about make out the words crackling over the line. "But I wanted to make sure . . . very hard for you . . . Jay's death . . ."

"Mom, I really can't hear you," I said. "I'll e-mail you later, okay?"

"Okay, darling. Just be brave, all right? We'll be home in no time."

"Just have a good vacation, Mom," I said. "Don't worry about me—I'm fine."

I rolled my eyes as I hung up the phone. This was why I shouldn't try to speak to her about Jay. Why did everyone have to overreact so much? It was like I wasn't even allowed to be upset about my best friend dying.

When Piper came to my room around six to tell me they were all heading down to the beach, I felt a sudden urge not to go, but couldn't think of any suitable excuse, especially since Piper had said that I was the only reason she was still allowed to go in the first place. Unfortunately, the weather forecast had been accurate and the wind had died down as the afternoon wore on.

I was just putting a few things into a bag when Lilias came into my room.

"Rebecca says I have to give you the rest of the message," she said, looking cross. "She says it's important. You got all weird and wouldn't let me finish last time, but she says you need to look on your phone. He left something for you on it that you have to see."

"Who?"

"Your friend. The one who died. The one who asked Rebecca to give you the message. She says she promised him that she would."

Lilias didn't give me a chance to reply, she just took off and left me staring after her. I picked up my phone, but then Piper called me from downstairs, so I stuffed it into my pocket and went to join her.

We took the clifftop steps down to the beach, with its smooth carpet of black sand. Brett was already there with another guy named Kyle and a couple of girls Piper knew from school.

Piper seemed to change as soon as she was with her friends.

When she introduced me, she said, "This is my cousin, Sophie. She's okay, really. You're just a little bit of a Goody Two-Shoes, aren't you?" She smiled at me as if this was all a joke.

The other two girls—Gemma and Sarah—were both effortlessly pretty, even if they were nowhere near as stunning as Piper. They annoyed me as soon as I met them, and it was obvious from the start that they didn't like me. Gemma had actually turned up wearing great big platform heels, which seemed a stupid choice for camping on the beach, as she kept falling over. In the end, Kyle picked her up and carried her, giggling, down the sand to where we set up the tents.

When we got the fire going and started cooking some food, I thought, for about half a minute, that maybe the night wouldn't be a total disaster after all. But then Piper suggested that we get changed into our pajamas.

I got dressed in the tent, then went to brush my teeth. When I came back, the other girls were sitting around the fire. They were all wearing silk nighties with lacy trims, and when they saw my sheep pajamas they fell over laughing, and no one laughed louder than Piper.

"Oh dear, Sophie, you really are quite the baby still," she said sweetly. "What are we going to do with you?"

I forced myself to grit my teeth. Piper was acting as if we were friends and it seemed to me that she was being careful to be not quite nasty enough. If I said anything, I knew it would look like I was overreacting. I had no choice but to go along with it.

"It's like looking at a six year old!" Gemma squealed. "Don't they have any grown-up pajamas in England?"

Have they only got cheap nighties in Scotland? I wanted to say.

Instead, I gave her my brightest smile. "You should see my onesie," I said. "It's got unicorns on it."

I knew then that coming on the camping trip with them had been a mistake, but it was too late to turn back to the house now—it would make it look as if they'd chased me away, and I'd die before I gave them that satisfaction.

Brett got out a pack of cigarettes and passed it around the group. When they got to me, I handed them on without taking one. I wasn't surprised when Piper instantly drew attention to it by saying, "Haven't you even smoked a cigarette before?"

"No, and I don't want to, thanks," I said, struggling to keep my voice level.

I was trying very hard not to think about Jay because this entire evening was making me miss him badly. As the others started to talk about some party they'd been to a few weeks before, I couldn't resist taking out my phone and scrolling through the photos, looking for whatever it was that Lilias had mentioned back at the house.

Suddenly, a photo came up that I didn't remember ever seeing before.

It was Jay in my bedroom, taking a selfie with my phone. And, right away, I knew what day this was because I could see the toffee cake we'd bought from the supermarket on the way home. It was the day he had asked me to go to the end-of-school dance with him and I'd laughed. Shortly afterwards I'd gone downstairs to get us some plates and Jay must have taken the opportunity to grab my phone. He was smiling into the camera and holding up a piece of paper he'd scribbled a message on:

I wasn't joking, silly.
And I'm going to ask you again.

For long moments I stared at the photo.

I won't cry, I told myself, *I absolutely will NOT cry*.

I knew I'd have to at some point, but not here, not now, in front of these people who were not my friends. But why would Rebecca have wanted me to see the photo? She was a vengeful, evil spirit. She was responsible for what had happened to Jay. Wasn't she?

"This is getting a little boring," Piper announced suddenly, bringing me back to reality. "Let's liven things up a bit. How about truth or dare?"

I knew from the start that this was going to be trouble, but the others all seemed into it. I put my phone back in my bag and waited nervously until it was my turn.

"Truth or dare?" Piper said, smiling at me. The light from the fire threw strange shadows over her perfect features so that, for once, she didn't look pretty at all. Her Frozen Charlotte necklace was in full view now that it wasn't hidden beneath a T-shirt, and I felt like the doll's eyes were staring right at me.

"Truth," I said, hoping that would be the least painful.

"Have you ever been kissed?" Piper said at once.

I felt myself blushing furiously in the dark. "No."

"That's no big surprise with pajamas like that!" Sarah laughed, while I wished the sand would just swallow me up.

"Oh, I dunno." Brett, who was sitting between Piper and me, leaned over and nudged my arm. "Some guys like sheep." He then looked a bit confused by what he'd just said. His tiny eyes appeared even smaller in the firelight, and I pulled away from his touch.

Piper was still looking at me. "Is that the truth?" she asked. "You've honestly never kissed anyone?"

"No," I said, wishing she would just drop it.

"I thought perhaps Jay . . . ?" she prompted.

"Who's Jay?" Gemma asked.

I didn't think I could handle it if they started talking about him. "No, I told you—"

"Yes, yes, he asked you to the school dance and you laughed in his face," Piper said, waving her hand as if it were nothing.

"Wow, that's harsh!" Kyle said.

I glared at Piper. "You know it wasn't like that."

"Sorry, Jay," Piper said, in a voice that was a shockingly accurate imitation of my own, "but, you see, I'd rather die than go to the dance with you."

Cameron's words from yesterday came back to me suddenly: *Piper is an excellent mimic . . .*

It really was like hearing my own voice coming out of someone else's mouth. Whatever game she was playing here, I didn't like it. Not one bit.

"You know what I think about Jay?" Piper asked, switching back to her own voice. "I think that he—"

"I don't want to know what you think about Jay," I said. "I don't want to hear you speak about him at all."

Everyone was staring at me. One of the other girls giggled, but I ignored her. My eyes were fixed firmly on Piper.

"Oh, settle down," she said, not seeming at all concerned. "Can't you take a joke?"

"Not about this," I said coolly. "Not about him."

"All right, all right, we won't talk about Jay anymore if it's going to kill the mood like this. Geez. It must be my turn by now anyway?"

"Truth or dare?" I said, before anyone else could beat me to it.

Her green eyes glittered in the firelight. "Truth."

I looked right at her, my heart thumping fast in my chest as I summoned the courage to ask my question. "What happened to Cameron's piano?"

I'd thought Piper might be angry. After all, even asking the question was pretty much an accusation against her boyfriend. But instead, she looked delighted. "Well, it's quite simple," she said, beaming. "I took it apart, piece by piece."

It was obvious by the silence that none of the others

had known this. For a moment, the crackle of the fire and the lapping of the waves on the sand nearby were the only sounds.

Then Gemma gave an uncertain laugh. "Wow, Piper, that's cold. Wasn't that piano worth a fortune?"

Brett seemed less amused. "What the hell, Piper?" he snapped. "I got dragged in by the police over that bloody thing. Why didn't you say anything? I could have gone to prison!"

"Oh, don't overreact," Piper said. "*You're* not going to prison."

She put a weird emphasis on "you're," almost like she thought someone else would be going to prison instead.

"Why did you do it?" I asked.

"No, you don't," Piper said, wagging her finger at me. "That's two questions. No freebies!"

"Who cares anyway?" Kyle said. "It's Brett's turn."

"Truth or dare, Brett?" Piper said, turning to her boyfriend.

After what Piper had just said, he didn't look much like he wanted to play anymore—his big shoulders were all hunched and he was sort of slumped in the sand like an ape having a sulk. "Dare," he grunted.

"Ooh, good choice," Piper said. She tapped her finger against her cheek and made a big show of trying to come up with something. Finally she said, "I've got it! Brett, I dare you to give Sophie her first kiss!"

"No thanks," I said, already leaning back.

"Sure, why not?" Brett said, glaring at Piper. With those tiny piggy eyes and sulky mouth I wondered how anyone could find him handsome. "Maybe she'll appreciate me more than you do."

Before I could stop him, he lunged towards me and pressed his mouth to mine.

It was a wet, slimy sort of kiss. His lips mashed roughly against my own and I could taste cigarette smoke on my tongue. Whenever I'd thought about what my first kiss would be like, I'd never imagined it would be as horrible as this. I shoved his chest hard with both hands to get him off my face. Then I slapped him. Hard.

"Don't ever touch me again," I said.

Kyle laughed. "That's you being told, man!"

Brett glared at me and, for a moment, I really thought he was going to punch me. But then he just said, "What the hell is your problem?"

"It's only a game, Sophie." Piper said. But we both knew that it wasn't.

"I don't want to play it anymore," I said. "I'm going to bed."

I got up and went into the tent I was sharing with Piper and the other girls. I wiped at my mouth angrily, wishing that I'd brought some mints so that I could get that disgusting taste out of my mouth. I was shaking with anger and didn't think I'd be able to sleep, despite the fact that I'd gotten so little the night before. I lay awake in my sleeping bag for a while, listening to them giggling together out there in the dark and sure that, whatever the joke was, it was at my expense.

Cameron had been right about Piper—there was something wrong with her. I thought about what Pat Jones had said about the dolls and wondered whether they could be somehow responsible for her behavior.

The others went to bed not long after me. I pretended to be asleep when Piper, Gemma, and Sarah came into the tent, and, after a bit of giggling and fidgeting around, they finally went to sleep, and so did I.

At some point during the night I opened my eyes and thought I saw someone outside. It was Cameron, standing on the other side of the glowing embers of the fire, staring off down the dark beach. Then he turned his head right towards me and our eyes seemed to meet for a moment through the last glow of the dying fire.

I sat up, rubbing my eyes in confusion and peering through the open flap of the tent, but the beach was dark and deserted and I couldn't see Cameron anywhere. Perhaps I'd dreamed it. Why would he be down here on the beach in the middle of the night, anyway?

I lay back down and slept until the early hours of the morning, when something woke me for real. Pale light streamed through the open door of the tent; the other girls were still asleep around me and I could hear the ocean lapping at the beach outside.

At first, I thought the voices I heard were the waves whispering against the sand, but then I heard the words, only barely audible beneath the soft rumble of the sea.

"Charlotte is cold . . ."

"Charlotte is cold . . ."

"Sophie? Sophie?"

"We want to play with you . . ."

"Charlotte is cold . . ."

"Let's play the Freezing-to-Death Game!"

"No, no, let's play the Stick-a-Needle-in-Your-Eye Game!"

"My favorite!"

There was muffled giggling, childish and high-pitched and, somehow, slightly insane.

And that was when the screaming started.

There was panic in that scream, and fear too, but mostly there was pure agony. The mindless shrieks of someone in terrible, excruciating pain.

The other girls were awake now, jerking upright in their sleeping bags and staring around at each other.

"What's going on?"

"Who's screaming?"

"Is that *Brett*?"

We stumbled out of the tent together, just in time to see Brett come staggering out of the boys' tent with both hands over his eyes. Kyle was right behind him, his face completely white.

Since he couldn't see where he was going, Brett stumbled almost at once and fell to his knees in the sand. He wasn't screaming anymore but crying instead, demented sobs that slobbered up out of his mouth.

"Brett, what *is* it?" Piper asked, rushing over to him.

It was already a warm morning but I felt cold all over as I noticed the thin lines of blood trickling down between Brett's fingers.

"My eyes!" he said, his voice thick and wet-sounding. His big shoulders heaved in another sob. "I can't see!" Blood ran down his hands and landed in big, fat drops on the beach, where they were instantly gobbled up by the black sand.

"We were asleep," Kyle said. "We were asleep and then he just . . . he suddenly started screaming like that."

"Let me see what's happened," Piper said.

Brett just knelt hunched there in the sand, shaking his head and moaning and even rocking himself a little. Gemma and Sarah stared at him, their mouths open in shock.

"Let me see," Piper said again, and she grabbed his hands and pulled them away.

We all cried out when we saw his face. Gemma, inexplicably, actually turned and ran off down the beach. Perhaps she thought whoever had done this to Brett might still be hiding in the tent somewhere.

Spit dribbled from Brett's mouth, and tears and blood mixed together on his cheeks. Both his eyes were closed and he couldn't have opened them even if he'd wanted to—his eyelids were pinned shut by the needle sticking out of each eye.

SIXTEEN

He called her once, he called her twice,
She answered not a word.
He asked her for her hand again,
And still she never stirred.

The ambulance couldn't get to the beach, so the paramedics had to climb down the clifftop steps with the stretcher. Brett looked so pathetic slumped there on his knees in the sand, crying and groaning, reaching out blindly to the paramedics with his bloodstained hands.

"Help me," he moaned. "Please help me."

"How did this happen?" one of the paramedics asked, looking us over as if one of us had shoved the needles into Brett's eyes as some kind of prank.

We all stared back at them in silence until Piper made me jump by suddenly bursting into tears.

"I don't want to get anyone in trouble," she said. "But . . . But I think I saw my brother down on the beach last night. He thought Brett destroyed his piano and he was so angry about it. I was afraid of what he might do . . ."

The paramedics exchanged glances as they strapped Brett onto the stretcher. "You'd better go home," one of them said. "And tell your brother to stay where he is for now."

After the paramedics had taken Brett away, the rest of us cleared up the campsite as quickly as we could. No one said anything. We just worked in silence. I was too furious to speak to Piper. She knew full well that Cameron had had nothing to do with what had happened to Brett, and yet she'd pointed the finger at him anyway.

I went into the boys' tent and it was immediately obvious which sleeping bag and pillow had been Brett's because of the bloodstains smeared across the white pillow. There were even a few drops of blood on the sides of the tent.

I shivered and reached down to pick up Brett's sleeping bag. I meant to roll it up but something fell out of it, landing on the sand with a thump. Frowning, I peered down at it. The moment I realized what the white object was, I recoiled, my heart beating fast in my chest.

It was a Frozen Charlotte, lying on her back on the black sand. One of her legs was broken at the ankle and the other was snapped off at the knee, but she had both her arms, bent at the elbow, with her tiny hands stretched up in front of her.

It was hard to say what was more horrifying about the doll—the fact that both her hands were covered in blood that ran all the way down her white porcelain arms, or the fact that she was smiling. While most of the Frozen Charlottes had pursed little rosebud mouths, this one had an impossibly huge smile, stretched and grotesque, like the smile of a clown that looked like it was about to split her head in two.

I don't want to go blind, do you? Lilias had said to me just a couple of nights ago. *Lock your door if you don't want to end up like that girl in the photo.*

I swallowed hard and, being careful to avoid touching the Frozen Charlotte, reached back down for Brett's sleeping bag and pulled it off the ground.

The moment I did so, I almost dropped it again in shock. When I picked it up I'd expected to see a smooth stretch of sand where it had been lying but, instead, there were hands. A whole forest of white hands sticking up out of the black sand, tiny fingers curled like claws. I remembered the feeling of being pinched, scratched, and grabbed by all those hands in the dream I'd had my first night at the house. My own breathing suddenly seemed very loud in my ears. Somewhere in the tent, somebody giggled, then quickly smothered it.

Piper came into the tent behind me a moment later. "Oh," she said brightly. "How did *they* get there?"

I looked at her and she smiled at me, a smile you could cut yourself on. I watched as she knelt down and dug away the soft sand to reveal the dark heads of the Frozen Charlotte dolls, like digging white corpses up out of the mud. And, all the while, Piper was humming to herself the soft, sweet lilt of the "Fair Charlotte" ballad.

"I . . . I'm just going to take this stuff back up to the house," I said, backing out of the tent.

Piper didn't reply and I left her there, scrabbling about in the sand with the dolls.

I was out of breath by the time I got to the house and my hands fumbled with the lock on the gate. I wanted to get in and speak to Cameron before Piper returned. He must have seen me from a window because he was already coming down the drive to meet me when I walked through the gate.

"I saw her," he said, before I could say anything. "I saw Rebecca last night."

There were dark circles under his eyes and he looked like he hadn't slept at all.

"Where?" I asked.

"I heard her, calling for help on the clifftop." He shook his head as if he could hardly believe what he was saying. "I was in the hall last night after everyone had gone to bed. Shellycoat was in there with me when she suddenly started to hiss and all her fur puffed up. I thought she was staring at nothing at first but then I saw her. I saw Rebecca. She was outside the house, staring straight through the window at me. She pressed her hand up against the glass and it was frozen—her skin was all cracked and white, like . . . like one of those awful dolls."

"So what happened?"

"I called out to her but she turned away from the window and walked out of sight. When I ran outside I couldn't see her, but I heard her for a little while. She was calling for help—her voice sounded raw, as if she'd been calling for hours." Cameron ran his hand through his hair and looked in the direction of the cliff. "I tried to find her but I lost her out there in the dark somewhere. I thought perhaps she'd gone down to the beach, but she wasn't there. I went back up to the clifftop and searched everywhere, but she was gone." He looked at me and said, "You were right. Rebecca really has come back."

"Listen," I said. "Something happened on the beach this morning. I don't think we have much time. Brett started screaming and then he came staggering out of the tent with needles shoved in both of his eyes. Piper told the paramedics that she saw you there last night."

"Oh God," Cameron said. "She's setting me up. This

whole thing with Brett and the piano and that night at the party have all been a setup. She wanted to make me the perfect suspect if anything should happen to Brett." He shook his head. "I knew something awful would happen to him if he stayed with Piper long enough. I just didn't know what."

"Is that why you attacked him that night?"

"I didn't know what else to do," Cameron said, so quietly it was almost a whisper. "I didn't know how else to protect him. I'd tried warning him off but that only made him more determined to be with her. So I thought that if I frightened him away then he might be safe. But that was what Piper wanted me to do all along."

"How dangerous is she?" I asked, dreading the answer. "How far would she actually go?"

Cameron looked right at me and I could see exhaustion in his eyes. "I don't know," he said. "I just don't know. After what happened with Rebecca—first the fire and then the clifftop—I always suspected, I always wondered and worried, but I could never be *sure*. Not completely. I love her, you know, that's the worst part of all this. Even after everything that's happened, even when I hate her, Piper's still my sister. I remember what she was like before and I just wish she could go back to being that person. It's like, one day something inside her just broke. She isn't right in the head anymore."

"I think it's because of the Frozen Charlotte dolls," I said.

Cameron groaned. "Not the dolls again! Why is everyone so obsessed with those horrible old things?"

"Think about it. When did Piper's behavior start to change? And what about Rebecca? When did she start behaving badly? I bet it was after they discovered the dolls and brought them up out of the basement, wasn't it?"

Cameron thought about it for a moment, then shrugged. "I guess it might have been around that time."

I repeated everything Pat Jones had told me about the dolls, and how I'd heard them whispering through the walls and scratching at the glass, and about the ones that had mysteriously turned up on the beach.

"I know it sounds insane," I said. "But it also explains a lot of things too. There've been too many deaths and accidents and injuries around the dolls for it to just be a coincidence. And I've heard them. I've heard them speak with my own ears."

"I don't know," Cameron said. "I don't know what to think. But even if you're right, what can we do about it?"

We didn't get the chance to talk further because the blue flash of a police car's light announced their arrival at the house and, a moment later, the officers were hammering at the gate.

Cameron looked at me. "They'll want to take me," he said. "If they think I'm responsible for what happened to Brett then . . ." He trailed off and I felt a chill of fear as my mind raced ahead. Brett had lodged an official complaint about Cameron attacking him with a riding crop. Then Cameron's priceless piano had been destroyed, and the police already knew he thought Brett was responsible. And then, just a few days later, Brett turns up blinded on a beach only a few meters away from where Cameron lived. He could end up going to prison for a very long time.

Cameron grabbed my arm suddenly and said, "Please don't leave. I'm sorry, I know I've got no right to ask you to stay, but please don't go away and leave Lilias here on her own. Piper's always known that I've suspected her and I think perhaps she's been more careful, more restrained, because of it. That's probably why she's gone to so much trouble to get me out of the way. She must have started this plan months ago when she first started dating Brett. If I'm not here to watch over her then God knows what will happen. Dad's useless—I've tried to tell him what Piper's like but he won't listen. I don't think he can accept it. After Rebecca died and Mom broke down, he couldn't take anything else. This isn't your problem and I've got no right to ask you, but please promise me that you won't leave Lilias here on her own."

His hand was tight around my arm and, as I looked up at him, I knew there was only one answer I could possibly give him. "I promise."

"She'll have a plan for you too," Cameron said. "I don't know what, but she will have thought of something. You must be careful."

I nodded. And then the gate was opened from the outside as Piper let the policemen in.

"Didn't you hear them knocking?" she asked. She wiped a tear from her eye and said, "Oh, Cameron. They've come to arrest you."

SEVENTEEN

He took her hand in his,
Oh God! T'was cold and hard as stone.
He tore the mantle from her face,
Cold stars upon it shone.

The police said that they weren't actually arresting Cameron, not yet anyway, but they were detaining him at the police station, which seemed to amount to the same thing. When Uncle James came out and realized what was going on, he asked to see a lawyer right away, but the police wanted to take statements from Piper and me, so Uncle James put Lilias in the car and took us all down to the station first.

We were taken to separate interview rooms and asked to go through what had happened. The policemen wanted to know what time we had arrived at the beach, what time we had gone to bed, and what had happened when Brett started screaming. Eventually one of them asked me the question I'd been dreading: "Was Cameron Craig on the beach last night?"

I didn't know how to answer that. After all, I couldn't say that he had been there chasing the ghost of his dead sister. And if I couldn't tell them the real reason why he was there, then they would surely assume he'd been there to attack Brett. He already had a motive as far as they were concerned. And if they could place him at the scene of the crime as well, then it would look really bad for him.

So I did something I never imagined I would do in a situation like this. I lied to a policeman. "No, he wasn't," I said.

The officer laid down his pen and glanced at his colleague. "You're sure?" he said, looking back at me. "You never saw Cameron Craig anywhere near the vicinity of the beach last night or the early hours of this morning?" He spoke gently enough, but I could tell he didn't believe me.

"It's okay if you saw him," the other one said. "You won't get into trouble as long as you tell us the truth."

"I never saw him," I said. "I had woken up a few minutes before Brett started screaming and I never saw anyone near his tent. If Cameron had done it, he would have had to run away pretty quickly, wouldn't he? I would have seen him on the beach, running back up the steps to the clifftop. We all would have seen him—we were out of our tents within seconds. He couldn't have got out of our sight that fast. He wasn't there."

"You don't think he could have been hiding on the beach somewhere and gone back to the house after the commotion died down?"

I shook my head. "Those steps in the cliff face are the only way up. Someone would have seen him."

"What happened when Brett came out of the tent?"

"We all came out of our tents too, and then Piper went over to him and pulled his hands away from his face."

"And that's when you realized he had needles in both his eyes?"

"Yes."

"That must have been extremely shocking for you."

"It was."

"So when you first came out of your tents, you were all looking at Brett?"

"Yes, he was screaming. We didn't know what was wrong with him at first."

"In that case," the policeman said, "you can't be absolutely sure that Cameron wasn't there, can you? You can't be certain that he didn't run up the steps while you were all looking the other way?"

"But that's not what happened."

"You don't believe that's what happened," the other policeman replied. "But you don't *know*. Do you? You can't know if anyone fled the scene if you were looking away from the only access point to the beach."

"I wasn't looking at the steps," I said, hating that I had to admit it, "but I—"

"Okay, Sophie, that answers my question. Thank you."

It was a horrible interview. I felt like they were trying to trick me into incriminating Cameron somehow. When it was finally over, we weren't allowed to see him, so Uncle James drove Lilias, Piper, and me back to the house. He'd managed to find a lawyer on the mainland who specialized in defending this kind of case, so he was going to get the ferry from Armadale to meet with him.

"I'll hopefully be back in time for dinner," he said. "As long as this wind doesn't get any worse. I'll let you know when I've caught the ferry. Oh, and Sophie, with all the commotion this morning, I forgot to tell you. Your mother called earlier. They're cutting their trip short. They'll be back by tomorrow and they're coming here to fetch you."

"Fetch me?" I repeated. "But why? Has something happened?"

Uncle James looked uncomfortable. "I think they just want to be with you right now," he said. "You can talk all that over with them when they get here. Now I must go or I'll miss the ferry. If you need anything, just call me."

And he drove off, leaving the three of us alone by the gate.

Piper was the first to speak. "Well," she said, her voice bright with false cheerfulness, "who's hungry? Why don't I make us some sandwiches since we missed lunch?"

She turned to unlock the gate, and Lilias and I exchanged dark looks behind her back. To my surprise, Lilias took my hand as we walked down the path towards the house.

As we opened the front door and stepped inside, Dark Tom greeted us from his cage with a shrill *"Cross my heart and hope to die, stick a needle in my eye!"*

Lilias shuddered beside me and I wished that horrible bird could have picked something, anything, else to say.

"Do you want cheese sandwiches or tuna?" Piper asked.

"I'm not hungry," Lilias replied quietly. "Neither am I," I said.

"I'll do tuna," Piper said, as if she hadn't heard us. She walked off to the kitchen and Lilias and I exchanged a glance before going upstairs. Lilias was still holding on to my hand and, when we got to the landing, she tugged me down the hall towards her bedroom.

As soon as the door closed behind us she said, "Piper's written you a letter. It's a secret letter."

"Why would she do that?" I asked. "She can speak to me, she doesn't need to write me a letter."

Lilias just shrugged. "I don't know. But Rebecca told me to tell you about it. She says you need to read it."

"Where is it?"

"In Piper's room."

"Where in her room?"

"I don't know. Do you want me to stand guard while you look for it? I have to tell you something first, though."

She stared up at me and, although Lilias always looked serious, this time she looked like someone had died.

"It's all right," I said. "Whatever it is, you can tell me."

"It's . . . It's about Cameron's piano." Her lower lip started to tremble.

"It's okay, I already know who broke it."

Her eyes went huge. "You do?"

"Yes, Piper admitted to us last night that she did it."

Lilias scowled. "Piper didn't do it," she said. "She just said that to shock everyone. Piper loves shocking people. It's one of her favorite things."

I frowned. "But if it wasn't Piper who broke the piano, then who did?"

Lilias took a deep breath and clenched her fists at her sides. "It was me," she said. "I did it." Tears suddenly filled her eyes. "I'm sorry," she whispered. "I'm sorry, I'm sorry. I knew it was wrong. The dolls kept telling me to go downstairs and do it at night after everyone else had gone to sleep but I said no, I wouldn't do that to my brother. He loves me just the way I am, he says I don't have to change if I don't want to." The tears were spilling down her cheeks now and she was trembling from head to toe. "Cameron's my favorite person in the whole world," she said. "And he told me that I'm his favorite person in the whole world too. I would never make him sad. Never, ever, ever. If one of us had to be sad I would want it to be me, not him. But that night it was like I couldn't help it. I couldn't stop. They just kept whispering and whispering at me and twisting it all up in my head. So I did it, even though I promised myself that I wouldn't. And when Cameron finds out he's going to hate me forever and I won't be his favorite person anymore."

"I think you'll always be his favorite person." I went and knelt on the floor in front of her. "He'll never hate you."

I put my arms around her and she threw her arms around my neck and hugged me tightly.

"We'll explain to Cameron what happened," I said. "You've known all along that there's something wrong with the Frozen Charlottes, haven't you? And I think Cameron might be starting to believe it too."

"Is that why Piper does such horrible things some-times?" Lilias asked, her voice muffled in my shoulder. "Because the dolls tell her to do it?"

"I don't know. But we're going to find out. And yes, if you can keep an eye out for her while I'm in her room that would really help me a lot."

"Okay," Lilias said, pulling back and wiping her eyes with her sleeve.

"Come on then," I said, giving her hand a squeeze. "Let's see if we can find this letter Rebecca is talking about."

Lilias went and stood watch at the top of the stairs while I let myself into Piper's room and looked around, wondering where to start.

My eye fell on the desk right away so I went over to it and started pulling open drawers. The first two seemed to be full of makeup and lotions, but the last one was locked and wouldn't budge when I tried to open it. I couldn't see a key anywhere so I did a quick sweep of the rest of the room but found nothing out of the ordinary.

I knew there wasn't much time until Piper came back upstairs so I took a risk and forced the drawer open with a ruler I found in one of the other drawers. Piper would know I'd been in her room but there wasn't time to be gentle about it.

I pulled open the locked drawer, not sure what I would see. There was just a notebook in there, and I thought it might be a diary at first, but when I pulled it out, a loose page fell from it.

I snatched it up and was surprised to see my own handwriting. It was the letter Piper had dictated to me a couple of days ago to her friend Sally. I frowned at it, wondering why she hadn't mailed it. Then I flipped open the notebook.

To my surprise, the first page was an exact copy of the letter to Sally, only this time it was in Piper's writing rather than mine. I quickly flipped through the other pages and felt my blood run cold. It was the same letter, written over and over again, only, as it went on, Piper's writing became more and more like my own, as if she was trying to copy it. Until, finally, her handwriting looked exactly the same as mine.

It must have taken her several hours of practice to get it right and I couldn't think why she would bother, until I flipped farther into the notebook and found another letter tucked right at the back.

This was the letter Lilias must have been talking about. Only Piper hadn't written it to me, she'd written it *as* me. It was my own handwriting scrawled across the page, even though I'd never seen it before.

I read through it and felt my breath leave my body like it had been sucked out. I sat down on the edge of Piper's bed with my hand clapped over my mouth.

It was a suicide note.

And it had my name signed at the bottom.

EIGHTEEN

Then quickly to the glowing hall,
Her lifeless form he bore.
Fair Charlotte's eyes were closed in death,
Her voice was heard no more.

I can't take it anymore. It's my fault that Jay died and I don't want to be here if he's not. Please tell my parents that I love them—and that I'm sorry.

Sophie

For a long moment I just stared at the note in my hand, reading it and rereading it, hardly able to believe what I was seeing.

She'll have a plan for you too, Cameron had said. But I had never thought that she would actually want to kill me. I thought back to those schoolgirls and the teacher who had died and wondered whether the Frozen Charlottes really could persuade one person to kill another. I knew that Lilias dearly loved Cameron and would never willingly do anything to hurt him, and yet she had destroyed the thing he prized the most.

I knew suddenly what I had to do—I had to get the dolls out of the house, every last one of them.

But there was something else I had to do first. I ripped the suicide note into shreds and stuffed the pieces into my pocket, then I took out my phone and tried to call Mom, but her phone was switched off and I guessed she must be flying. So I called the home number instead. I knew no one would be there but I wanted to leave a message on the answering machine. If anything were to happen to me then I needed them to know that it wasn't suicide, that I would never do that to myself, or to them.

But, to my surprise, I couldn't leave a message because an electronic voice informed me that the answering machine was full. I frowned. How could we possibly have received so many messages in such a short amount of time? I keyed in the password to listen to them and, as soon as the first message started to play, I knew that my life really was in serious danger.

It was my own voice on the machine. The first message had been left the night I arrived at the house, and I listened in horror to the sound of myself crying and saying that it had been a mistake to go to Skye and that I felt more lonely and depressed than ever. As the messages went on they became worse and worse. I listened to my voice telling my parents that I had never felt so unhappy before and that I just wanted the pain to stop.

I'd heard Piper mimic my voice before but this was something else altogether. And the worst thing about it was that she'd left the first message just hours after meeting me when I arrived at the house. She must have planned this from the start. She'd meant to do me harm from the moment she met me. We had never been friends.

I couldn't stop my hands from shaking. Would my parents actually believe that I would kill myself? Surely they knew me better than that? But with my own voice leaving those messages on the answering machine, what else were they supposed to think?

My only chance was to get the dolls out of the house and hope that would be enough to stop Piper. "The sandwiches are ready!" she called from downstairs at just that moment.

I snatched up her notebook. Then I noticed her bag by the door and yanked it open to look inside. A collection of broken dolls stared back at me, their white skin stained with black sand. I took the bag back with me to my own room. Lilias hovered in the doorway, watching nervously as I pulled out my suitcase and dumped the Frozen Charlottes into it.

"What are you doing?" she asked.

"I'm getting rid of the dolls," I said, trying to sound more confident than I actually felt. "Can you stand watch for a few more seconds while I get the ones from Rebecca's room?"

Lilias's eyes had gone huge again, but she just nodded and went back to the top of the staircase.

I took the suitcase into Rebecca's room and went straight to the doll cabinet. The hateful little things were all lined up on their shelves, their pursed mouths and pinched expressions seeming to disapprove of me, and I was sure I recognized the tiny one that had bitten me lying on the bottom shelf.

But the moment I stood before the doll cabinet I remembered that it was locked. I ran over to the music box and snatched the key from inside, slamming the lid closed before the box could tinkle out more than a few notes of that creepy ballad.

I opened the cabinet and, without ceremony, started sweeping the Frozen Charlotte dolls into my case. Some of them cracked and broke as they fell in but I didn't care.

"What are you two doing up there?" Piper called. It sounded like she was right at the bottom of the staircase.

"We're just coming!" Lilias shouted back.

But I could hear footsteps on the stairs and I knew that Piper was coming up to see what we were doing. "Come on, come on!" I whispered to myself, my palms sweaty as I frantically gathered the rest of the dolls.

The bottom shelf was just a collection of limbs— broken legs and arms and heads. If these were ordinary dolls I would have left them there, but I didn't trust the legs not to go running around by themselves or the arms to pick up a needle or the heads to start whispering their hateful words of poison. So I swept them into the suitcase too and then grabbed the Frozen Charlotte music box and threw that in.

"I told you we were just coming," Lilias said out on the landing, and I knew she was trying to warn me that Piper was almost here.

I grabbed the suitcase and ran out of the room just as Piper climbed the last few stairs. She looked up at the two of us. "I'd started to think something had happened to you both," she said. Then she saw my suitcase and said, "Are you going somewhere, Sophie?"

"I just thought I'd get a head start on packing," I said. "Since my parents are coming tomorrow."

"So they are." Piper smiled, displaying her perfect white teeth. "We haven't got much time left, then. What a shame. Well, come on, these sandwiches won't eat themselves."

"Let me just stick this in my room," I said, indicating my suitcase.

I put it in my room, snapped the padlock closed around it, and put the key in my pocket before heading down to lunch. Piper had set three plates of sandwiches on the dining room table, which surprised me because she usually just made one big plate and we helped ourselves.

When Lilias reached out for one of the plates, Piper practically slapped her hand away. "Not that one!" she snapped. Lilias jumped back, looking startled, and Piper quickly smiled and said in a more normal voice, "I cut yours into triangles, just the way you like them. Here you go."

She handed her sister one of the plates and then picked up the plate that Lilias had tried to take to begin with and handed it to me. "This one's for you, Sophie."

I took the plate from her, suddenly feeling sick. Why was she so set on me having these particular sandwiches? What if she'd put something in them? It would be such a simple thing to mix some rat poison or something in with the tuna. Along with the suicide note and all those voice-mails, everyone would think I had deliberately overdosed. Whatever happened, I knew I must not eat the sand-wiches, or any other food Piper gave me.

I sat down with the other two at the table and said, "Have you heard any news about Brett?"

Piper normally ate her food in dainty bites, so I was surprised when she practically stuffed an entire sandwich in her mouth, swallowed it down, and said, "I called Brett's mom a little while ago. She said some surgeons operated on him earlier to try to save his eyesight."

"And did it work?" I asked when she didn't elaborate.

"Why, no," Piper said, picking up another sandwich and eyeing it with a greedy look. She took another huge bite, then carefully wiped the corner of her mouth with a napkin and said, "They had to remove both his eyes." She beamed around the table at us. "Isn't that tragic?"

"It's awful," I said.

"He's a blubbering mess, of course," she said. "And his mom's in a terrible state about it. You should have heard her boo-hooing to me on the phone. I thought she'd never shut up. Still, it will be some comfort to her when Cameron goes to prison, I suppose."

Lilias slammed her hand down on the table. "Cameron is *not* going to prison!" she said, glaring at Piper across the table.

"Oh, Lilias, don't be naive—of course he is," Piper said. "For a very long time. You'll be all grown up by the time he gets out, I expect. *If* he ever gets out, that is. Accidents happen in prison, so I hear."

"You're such a liar," Lilias muttered, scowling back down at her plate.

"Aren't you hungry, Sophie?" Piper asked, ignoring her sister's remark. "You haven't touched your sandwiches."

"I think I've lost my appetite," I said, pushing the plate away slightly.

"You ought to eat something, you know," Piper said. "You've had nothing since last night at the beach."

"I really couldn't," I said. "Not after what you just said about Brett."

"Wow, that kiss must have really affected you!"

"I'd feel the same way about anyone who lost their eyes!" I snapped. "Even someone I don't like."

"Whatever you say," Piper said with a smirk. "But if you don't want your sandwiches then I'm sure you won't mind if I give them to Shellycoat?"

The elderly cat had just come into the room and was purring and rubbing herself around my legs. When Piper grabbed one of my sandwiches and held it out to her, the old cat hobbled over eagerly.

"No, don't!" I said, slapping the sandwich from Piper's hand and snatching it up off the floor before Shellycoat could get to it. "There . . . There might be bones in it," I said, forgetting about Lilias's phobia for a moment.

"Bones?" Lilias looked suddenly ashen and pushed her plate away.

"You're right," Piper said slowly, an odd look in her eyes. "It could be dangerous."

For a moment we just stared at each other across the table.

"Well," Piper said finally. "Since we all seem to have suddenly lost our appetites, I might as well clean up."

"I think I'll go and finish reading my book," I said.

"Okay," Piper replied. "See you later, then."

Lilias and I went back upstairs and the moment we were alone I said, "Lilias, can you do something for me? I'm going to get rid of the Frozen Charlotte dolls and I need you to go to your bedroom, lock the door, and stay there until I get back, okay? Don't open the door for anyone. Not even Piper."

Lilias nodded slowly. "When you get back, how will I know that it's really you?" she asked. "Piper steals people's voices."

"Good point," I said. "We need a password. You pick one."

"Licorice," she said at once. "That's my favorite candy."

"All right, when I get back I'll say licorice and then you'll know it's me and you can let me in."

I watched Lilias go into her room and heard the click as she locked herself in. Then I grabbed the suitcase from my room and hurried back down the stairs, praying that Piper wouldn't appear.

Dark Tom eyed me from his perch and it was almost like he knew what I was about to do because he cocked his head and said, *"Frozen Charlotte? Dreadfully cold. Dreadfully cold."*

I didn't even pause to shush him, I just threw open the door and hurried down the garden path towards the gate.

NINETEEN

And there he sat down by her side,
While bitter tears did flow.
And cried, "My own, my charming bride,
You never more will know."

T he second I was outside the gate I started running
down the clifftop path, the suitcase full of broken
dolls thumping against my leg with each pounding step. I
could hear their delicate porcelain bodies clinking together
and I hoped they were breaking into a million pieces.

When I left the path and walked to the edge of the
clifftop, the dolls started to speak.

"Please don't hurt us . . ."

"Please, Sophie . . ."

"Let us out . . ."

"We'll be good, we promise . . ."

"Don't put us in the water . . ."

"Sophie, we just want to be your friends . . ."

"Your friends . . ."

"Your best *friends . . ."*

"Please, Sophie, let us out . . ."

"Take us back to the house . . ."

"We'll never tell . . ."

"Never . . ."

It was the weirdest thing but, even though I knew the dolls were evil and that I had to get rid of them, when they asked me to take them back, I felt the strongest desire to do it. I even took a step away from the cliff and towards the house, but then I shook my head, ridding myself of those horrid little whispers that were trying to make me do something I didn't want to.

I stepped back to the cliff edge and looked down at the dark waves pounding against the black rocks. Before they could find some way of stopping me, I lifted the suitcase over my head and threw it over the edge.

It sailed out away from the cliff in a perfect arc before finally hitting the water with a splash that created a small explosion of white foam. The waves picked the suitcase up and hurled it against the rocks a couple of times before it filled with water and slipped beneath the surface. I watched it go with a sense of satisfaction. The currents could carry it out to rest with the shipwrecks and the skeletons and the dead men's fingers—the Frozen Charlottes couldn't do any damage there.

I watched the water crashing against the rocks for another couple of minutes, but the suitcase didn't resurface, so I turned back towards the path, intending to head back to the house.

But, as I turned around, I saw the small white cross that had been put on the clifftop in memory of Rebecca. There was a little girl standing next to it. A girl wearing a white nightgown. She had her back to me and was looking out to sea, her long, dark hair trailing out behind her. I was sure it must be Rebecca but, when I called out to her, the wind snatched my voice away, and the little girl didn't turn around. She just stared out over the cliff with her arms hanging loosely by her sides.

I started down the path towards her, but had only gone a few steps when I walked into the most shocking cold spot. It seemed to wrap around me like a blanket, a biting, scratching, spiteful cold that went right through to my bones, scraping at them like scalpels. My eyes watered and my breath frosted before me.

"Rebecca!" I called again.

She still didn't react, so I carried on down the path. Finally I was right there behind her and, this time, when I said her name, she slowly turned around to face me. Her skin had a bluish tinge to it, all frozen and cracked, and her black hair was stiff with frost. Ice sparkled on her lips and her eyes had deep dark circles under them.

For a moment we just stared at each other in silence, but then she slowly reached her hand towards me. I hesitated, but Rebecca didn't seem dangerous standing there on the cliff. She just seemed sad and small and very alone. Now that I knew she'd been trying to tell me about the message Jay had left for me on my phone, I couldn't feel afraid of her as I had before. I reached out my hand to hers.

Her cold fingers curled around mine, just like they had that night at the café.

The instant our hands met, it was like my body disappeared. Suddenly it was nighttime and I found myself in Rebecca's head as she fell over the edge of the cliff. This wasn't a phantom Rebecca, but the living, breathing girl as she had been eight years ago. I felt the thump all the way through her bones when she landed on the rocky outcrop several feet below, heard the pained gasp that frosted the air before her in the dark, and felt the warmth of tears on her cheeks as she started to cry.

And then I heard Piper's voice from the clifftop above, calling Rebecca's name. The next moment her strawberry blonde head poked over the edge of the cliff and peered down, surrounded by a vast backdrop of stars that sparkled like little chips of broken glass in the night sky above her. She didn't look the same as she did now—she looked exactly as she had when we'd first met as children.

"Rebecca, are you okay?" Piper called down.

To my surprise, Rebecca scrambled carefully to her feet in the snow. "I . . . I think so," she said, pulling her coat tighter around her.

"Really?" Piper sounded more surprised than concerned.

But this wasn't right. Rebecca had broken her leg when she'd fallen—that was why she'd been unable to climb back up the cliff. And she hadn't been wearing a coat, only a nightgown. And she'd been alone—no one had ever said anything about Piper being with her.

"I told you we should have waited till tomorrow to come and fetch Charlotte!" Rebecca called.

I realized that she had a Frozen Charlotte clasped in her hand.

"But she was afraid and cold out here by herself!" Piper called back. "Is she still crying?"

Rebecca lifted the doll to her ear and, for the first time, I could hear a soft weeping over the sound of the ocean waves below.

"It's okay, Charlotte," Rebecca whispered. "Don't be scared. Soon we'll be back home in the warmth. I promise."

"Can you climb back up?"

"I don't know. It's really high!" Rebecca looked down over the ledge. It was a sheer drop to the scattered rocks hundreds of feet on the beach below. The wind blowing in from the sea tugged at her hair as if it was trying to pull her over the side. Rebecca pressed herself against the cliff face. "Maybe you should go and fetch Mommy!"

"But we'll get into trouble!" Piper called back. "It's not that high—you can climb it."

Rebecca looked again at the black beach yawning beneath her like the mouth of some awful monster, and I felt her wishing she had never let Piper talk her into coming out here like this in the first place.

"Rebecca, come *on*!" Piper called. "It's safe—don't be such a baby!"

Rebecca slipped the Frozen Charlotte into her coat pocket and then put both hands against the cliff face, searching for a hold. Fear of the drop below was making her legs feel shaky, but she counted to ten under her breath and then began to climb.

The freezing stone cut into her fingers but she dragged herself up anyway, using the ledges and footholds carved into the rock. Despite the freezing night air, I could feel the sweat running down her back by the time she finally reached the top, panting for breath, both arms trembling with the effort.

Letting Rebecca into my head and seeing that night through her eyes, I could feel her emotions as well and I sensed her shock of surprise and uncertainty when she reached the top and didn't find Piper crouched at the edge ready to help her, as she'd expected, but sat a little ways back from the clifftop, humming to herself and building a small snowman in the moonlight on the ground in front of her, as if she didn't realize her younger sister was clinging to the edge of a cliff for dear life.

"Piper!" Rebecca gasped. "Help me!"

Piper got up and wandered over to the cliff edge, still humming under her breath. It was a song I knew well by now—the "Fair Charlotte" ballad.

When she reached Rebecca she abruptly stopped humming and gave a sudden smile. "You know, if I wanted to, I could just kick you in the face right now and you'd fall all the way back down again."

"That's not funny!" Rebecca said, scowling at her. "Help me up!"

Still smiling, Piper shrugged and reached out to grab the hood of Rebecca's coat, but when she pulled, one of Rebecca's arms started to slip from her sleeve.

"Don't!" she yelled. "Don't pull on the coat—you'll pull it off!"

But Piper just seemed to pull even harder, until Rebecca's right arm had slipped out of the sleeve altogether.

I felt her heart speed up inside her chest as her fingers scrabbled to regain a hold on the clifftop.

"I said *stop*!" she shouted at her sister. "You're going to make me fall again!"

"Well, just pass me your coat," Piper replied. "I can't hold on to your arm if your sleeve is in the way, can I?"

Rebecca shrugged off the other sleeve and held the coat up to Piper, who snatched it and threw it on the ground.

"Now help me up," Rebecca said.

When Piper didn't reply straight away, Rebecca looked up and saw her sister staring down at her in the moonlight, a strange smile on her face.

"Piper—" Rebecca began, but that was as far as she got before Piper drew back her snow-crusted boot and kicked Rebecca hard in the face.

I felt Rebecca's lip split as blood poured into her mouth and smeared against her teeth. One of her fingernails ripped off as she lost her grip on the rock and fell back down the cliff face to the ledge below. She landed with a great thump that jarred every bone in her body and, at the same moment, a memory flashed clearly into her mind, a recent one from just that summer of standing in a burning tree house, screaming for help and wondering why Piper was just standing there in the garden watching the tree burn, and didn't run to fetch their mom and dad.

Without her coat, the frozen rock felt like knives beneath her nightgown. Knives that would peel her skin right off. A sob of pain and fear bubbled up out of Rebecca's chest as she slowly sat up on the ledge. "W-what did you do that for?" she cried, each breath frosting before her. With only her nightgown to protect her, the cold was almost unbearable. The frozen air made her lungs ache with the effort of breathing, and she couldn't prevent herself from shivering so violently that her bones seemed to rattle inside her body.

"Don't be such a crybaby, Rebecca!" Piper called down.

"Go and fetch Mommy!" Rebecca shouted back, no longer caring whether they were discovered out there.

"No, I'll get into trouble!" Piper said.

"But I'm s-s-so cold!"

"Tough!"

Rebecca started crying properly now. She'd never been so cold in her life. Her skin felt like it was bleeding and splitting in the raw air that was blasting in from the sea, crashing into her over and over again like relentless waves.

"Piper, please," she called. "Please help me!"

"Don't want to," Piper called back. Her voice was cheerful, as if this was just a game. That was what scared Rebecca most of all.

"But what if I freeze to death like Frozen Charlotte did?"

"I hope you do. I don't want a sister anymore."

"No!" Rebecca sobbed. "No, but, Piper, I don't want to be dead!"

"It's not so bad to be dead." The Frozen Charlotte doll whispered the words from the clifftop but, somehow, Rebecca still heard them over the pounding of the ocean. Perhaps the doll whispered them inside her head. *"It's not so bad to die."*

But Rebecca didn't believe her. She remembered what it had been like in the tree house before Cameron came to get her out. Trying to breathe, she'd sucked smoke into her lungs that squeezed around her throat and made her heart beat so fast she thought it was going to explode out of her chest. Rebecca didn't want to die.

So she wiped her tears away and reached her trembling hands back towards the cliff face. Blood ran down her finger where she'd torn away her nail, but she couldn't feel it through the cold. She was shivering so badly she was afraid she wouldn't be able to hold on, but she pulled herself up to the first foothold anyway.

"Don't you come up here!" Piper shrieked, seeing what she was doing. "No! No! I don't want you to! Go back down!"

Rebecca ignored her. She gritted her teeth against the icy wind that sheared her skin and tugged at her nightgown as if it was trying to drag her off the cliff. She reached up, feeling for something else to grab on to.

The next moment she cried out as a snowball hit the top of her head. It cracked like ice as it burst apart, and lumps of snow slid down her hair and the back of her neck, turning into icy fingers of water that trickled all the way down her spine.

"Piper, *stop it*!" she screamed.

She tried to carry on climbing, but Piper threw snowballs at her as fast as she could make them, and then she must have found some stones beneath the snow because she started throwing those too. They cut Rebecca's skin where they hit her, slicing it open to the raw sea air. One of the stones caught her just above her eye, and as blood dripped into her eyelashes, Rebecca lost her grip on the rock and fell all the way back down to the ledge.

This time, her weight landed on her right leg, and I heard the bone snap as it broke. Rebecca crumpled to the ground, the breath knocked out of her for a moment of pure, breathless agony before she screamed. The sound seemed to crack the frozen night air around them into shattered glass.

"Piper, my leg!" she shouted through streaming tears. "I've hurt my leg!"

"I've never been to a funeral before," Piper replied. "I wonder what it will be like? I wonder if everyone will cry? Do you think Mommy will buy me a new dress?"

Rebecca dragged herself into the corner between the cliff edge and the ground, as far away from the steep drop as she could get. She begged and pleaded with Piper until her throat was raw, but it did no good. Piper just giggled, as if they were playing a game.

"W-was it the . . . the Frozen Charlottes?" Rebecca asked between cracked lips and chattering teeth as she remembered all the bad and naughty things the dolls had ever told her to do. "Did they t-tell you to t-trick me out here like this?"

"No, the Frozen Charlottes didn't tell me!" Piper said. She sounded offended, as if the dolls were being given credit that should have rightly gone to her. "*I* told *them*! It was my idea to leave one of the dolls out here, just like it was my idea to set the tree house on fire."

I felt Rebecca's heart turn to stone when she heard this. There was silence for the first time since Rebecca had fallen over the edge of the cliff. Then Piper suddenly said, "I'm bored with this game, and I'm cold. I'm going back to bed. You can keep Charlotte." She threw the Frozen Charlotte doll back down the cliff and it shattered beside Rebecca in a pile of broken porcelain.

And that was it. Piper left and Rebecca was alone on the cliff. Her limbs felt like lead and each breath she took was like trying to breathe knives, but she reached over and picked up the doll's head—the largest surviving piece. The Frozen Charlottes told her to do bad things sometimes but I could feel how much love Rebecca had for the magical dolls that spoke to her and said they wanted to be her best, most special friends in all the world.

"*Shh,*" the Frozen Charlotte head whispered. "*It's not so bad to die. You'll get to play with us forever and ever.*" Rebecca tried to flex her fingers but the muscles had locked in place and it hurt to move them. She was afraid that if she tried to stand up she would fall over the edge of the ledge, hundreds of feet to the beach below. So she stayed where she was, a strange fog filling her head so that she couldn't be sure whether she sat there for hours or only minutes. It seemed like an eternity of staring down at the black sand shining in the moonlight and hearing Frozen Charlotte softly humming her ballad in the still, silent night.

At some point, Rebecca's heart began to feel strange. It was beating sluggishly at irregular intervals, all wrong and out of time in a way that made her chest ache. And then the strangest thing happened. The cold seeped away and she actually started to feel warm! A delicious warmth that spread all the way through her, a lovely, bright glow that made her drowsy and ready, at last, to lay her head back in the snow and sleep until someone came to rescue her.

And then she heard Piper's voice up on the clifftop, calling out to her and saying she was sorry, that she loved her and had brought help. She heard Cameron calling her name, and her mom and dad too. They'd come to get her. Rebecca felt a small explosion of joy deep inside her chest as she looked up and saw her parents, and her brother and sister, standing at the edge of the clifftop, smiling down at her. She tried to speak but only a hoarse croak came out.

And then she blinked and, suddenly, they were gone. There was no one on the clifftop. No one coming to rescue her. No one even knew she was there, except Piper. And Rebecca realized that Piper wasn't sorry; she was at home in bed, tucked up in the warmth, asleep. And she wasn't coming back.

A tear slowly ran down Rebecca's cheek as she closed her eyes and let her head fall back onto the snow. She breathed out slowly as her heart did a few more of those strange, sluggish beats, and then stopped.

TWENTY

He twined his arms about her neck,
He kissed her marble brow,
His thoughts flew back to where she said,
"I'm growing warmer now."

I gasped for air on the clifftop, my own heart racing in my chest as everything around me returned to normal. I felt chilled to my bones by what I'd just witnessed. I couldn't see Rebecca on the clifftop anywhere but I realized that this was what she'd wanted all along—for someone to know the truth about what happened to her. She hadn't died by accident. She'd been murdered by her own sister.

I thought suddenly of Lilias and knew I had to get back to the house. But when I turned around, Piper was standing on the path, just a few meters away, holding something behind her back. She smiled when she saw me looking at her.

"Hello, Sophie," she said. "You're not leaving, are you?"

"No, I just . . . I just went for a walk."

"Only I saw your suitcase was gone, so I thought perhaps you'd decided to go home without saying good-bye. And I can't let you do that. Oh, Sophie, I'm afraid we have a problem now that you've seen something you weren't supposed to."

"I don't know what you mean," I said, desperately trying to sound normal.

"Come on, now. We both know that's not true." Piper's voice softened suddenly. "You know, it would have been a lot easier for you, for everyone, really, if you'd never found that letter. It's made everything very messy. Not neat and tidy at all."

"What's that you're holding behind your back?" I asked.

"What . . . this? I unlocked the kitchen drawer." Slowly Piper drew out a huge meat knife, gleaming and sharp. She smiled. "The Frozen Charlottes want to play the Knife Murder Game."

"Piper—"

"Ready, set, *go!*"

She sprang at me like a cat, and I turned and ran. My first thought was to try to outrun her, either by going along the clifftop or taking off into the fields, but there was hardly any distance between us. She could catch up with me at any moment and bury the knife in my back. I could hear her footsteps crunching on the path behind me and could already feel the blade biting into my skin. So instead I ran to the only safe place in the area that I knew of—Rebecca's clifftop ledge.

For an awful moment as I lowered myself over the cliff, I thought I was going to miss the ledge, but I just made it. I managed to land on both feet, then the momentum drove me forward onto my hands and knees, so close to the edge that my fingers curled over it. My phone flew out of my pocket and I watched it skitter over the side to smash on the rocks below. I felt warm blood beneath my palms and realized I'd cut them when I fell, and both my knees throbbed. For a breathless second I gazed down at the black sand that Rebecca had sat staring at while she froze to death. Then I quickly scrambled away from the edge and pressed my back firmly up against the cliff face.

"Oh, not this again!" Piper's voice came from above me. "I'm not going to have to throw rocks at you too, am I?"

"You're insane!" I gasped.

"*I'm* insane?" She laughed. "You're the one clinging to the edge of a cliff. This seems a strange time to go rock climbing, I must say. Haven't you noticed that it's howling a gale?"

"What's wrong with you?" I stared up at her, wondering how I could have ever missed that deranged glint in her eye. There was something different about her face, as if a mask had been peeled away, revealing something rotten underneath. "How could you kill your own sister?"

Piper tilted her head a little. "Did Cameron tell you that?"

"No. Rebecca did. She showed me what happened."

Piper stared down at me. "Do you actually believe that? You really think you've seen Rebecca? You're as crazy as Lilias."

"I have seen her," I said. "I spoke to her through a Ouija board back home. She escaped from the board and came here with me."

Piper just smiled and shook her head. "So what's your plan? I mean, are you just going to stay down there forever?"

"I only need to stay here until your dad gets back."

"He's not coming back tonight. Didn't you hear? Because we took so long giving our statements at the police station, he arrived on the mainland too late to see the lawyer, so he's staying over and seeing him first thing in the morning. He phoned an hour ago to tell me. And, even if he wanted to come back, he couldn't. It's the wind, you see. They've had to close the bridge and cancel the ferries. There's no way on or off the island tonight."

"Well, it's not winter now," I said. "I can stay out here all night if I have to."

"*You* can," Piper replied sweetly. "But Lilias is back at the house."

"And how will you explain it if anything happens to Lilias?" I said. "I know you think you've got it all worked out for me with that fake suicide note and those voicemails you left for my parents, but don't you think people will be suspicious if your other sister dies under mysterious circumstances as well?"

"But they won't be mysterious circumstances," Piper said, smiling down at me. "Lilias has a phobia of bones, remember? You must have noticed her scar? You saw what she tried to do to herself once before. All I have to do is give Lilias a knife and she'll kill herself with almost no persuading at all. She's terrified of that skeleton inside her and would love nothing more than to cut it out. It would have worked the first time if Cameron hadn't poked his nose in. He's always ruining things. That's why I had to get him out of the way. He's chased away all my friends, but he can't chase away the Frozen Charlottes. They were the only ones who ever preferred me to Rebecca. Rebecca used to cry when they asked her to do things. And when she did what they told her to she was normally stupid enough to get caught doing it and would then whine about how it was the Frozen Charlottes' fault. I never did that. I've always been loyal to the dolls. And they've been better friends to me than any person ever has."

"Well, they're gone now," I said. "You'll never see them again."

"What the hell is that supposed to mean?"

"I packed them all in my suitcase," I said. "And threw them over the edge of the cliff."

Piper stared at me for a moment. "You're lying."

"I'm not lying. They're all gone. Every last one of them. I even took the broken arms and legs and heads. They'll be at the bottom of the sea by now."

She shook her head. "You're making it up. You're just trying to scare me." I saw her glance towards the house and then look back down at me. "You're just trying to get me to leave so that you can climb up from there and run off."

"The dolls are gone," I said. "They were evil little things that poisoned your house. I bet that's why someone tried to lock them away in the basement all those years ago. But now that they're gone you don't need to do the terrible things they told you to do anymore."

But even as I spoke I knew it wasn't going to work. Piper had one hand clasped to her throat, and I realized I hadn't got all the dolls after all—she still had her necklace. And even though it was only a head and some broken hands, it could still whisper vile words in her ear and put evil thoughts in her head.

Piper gripped the handle of the knife so hard that her knuckles turned white, and the look in her eyes as she glared down at me was simply demented. "I *liked* playing those games with the Frozen Charlottes!" she hissed. "I'm not like Rebecca, or Lilias; I don't play the game and then cry about it afterwards. I play the game and then ask the dolls when we can play it *again*. If you really have done something to them then I—" She seemed to choke on the words—she was so angry that she almost couldn't get them out. "If you're telling the truth," she tried again, "then you've just made the biggest mistake of your miserable life."

And, with that, she turned and stepped away from the clifftop, disappearing from sight. I had no way of knowing whether she'd just taken a few steps back and was still waiting for me, or whether she really had returned to the house to check on the dolls.

I remembered what I had told Lilias about locking the door to her room and staying there until I got back. With Cameron gone, she was all by herself, waiting for me. I'd promised I would stay with her and I knew what Piper had said was true—it wouldn't be difficult to hurt Lilias, and if Piper gave her a knife then she'd probably do it all by herself without too much persuading.

I reached for the rock and found ledges and footholds, just as Rebecca had done. The wind howled around me, tugging at my clothes and pulling at my hair, doing its very best to drag me right over the side of the cliff.

As I got close to the top, I hesitated for a moment. If Piper was still up there, then she'd be on me the moment my hands grabbed the side of the cliff. She could bring her knife down and cut my fingers off with one swipe, or stab the blade down full force into the top of my skull.

I swallowed hard, already imagining the blood soaking my hair, and reached my hand up for the edge of the cliff.

The second I did so, another hand clapped down on top of mine. I screamed and almost lost my grip. But it wasn't Piper staring down at me.

It was Cameron.

For a moment we just looked at each other in shocked silence. Then Cameron tightened his grip around my wrist and said, "Well, are you just going to hang there all day?"

With his help, I scrambled up onto the clifftop and moved away from the edge on shaky legs.

"What are you doing here?" I asked. "I thought—"

"The police can't hold me for more than six hours without charging me," he replied. He looked exhausted— the circles under his eyes were so dark they resembled bruises. "They haven't decided whether they're going to or not. I have to go back to the police station in the morning for more questions. I got the bus home, but as I was about to go inside I . . . thought I heard Rebecca again, calling for help. When I saw your hand come up over the edge like that, I . . . just for a second, I thought . . . What the hell are you doing out here like this anyway?"

"There's no time to explain," I said. "We've got to get back to the house. Piper came after me with a knife."

"A *knife*?" Cameron's face went suddenly ashen.

"She was with Rebecca that night. Somehow Rebecca showed me what happened. Piper was there and she left her to die. I threw the Frozen Charlottes into the sea—I thought that might release their hold over Piper and that she'd be, you know, normal again, but I don't think she ever *was* normal. I think she *likes* doing these awful things. And, Cameron, she was so angry when I said I'd gotten rid of them. And Lilias is in the house with her."

"Come on," Cameron said, already turning away. "We need to hurry."

We ran the whole way. I had a stitch in my side by the time we reached the gate, which Piper had locked behind her. The sun wouldn't set for some hours yet, but the overcast sky cast long shadows over everything and the house looked like an empty shell huddled there, with thin ribbons of sea mist curling around the bell tower.

There was total silence as we got closer and I realized that every single window was covered. The curtains were all drawn in the windows upstairs and it looked like sheets had been hung up over the downstairs ones.

Cameron turned to me and said, "Maybe you should stay outside. If Piper really has lost it—"

"I'm coming with you." I quickly cut him off. No way was I staying outside twiddling my thumbs, wondering about what might be happening inside.

To my surprise, Cameron reached for my hand, and his fingers wrapped warm and strong around mine. "Stay close beside me then," he said.

He gave my hand a squeeze and I squeezed back. Then we turned to the house and bolted up the steps to the front door together, both dreading what we might find inside.

TWENTY-ONE

He carried her back to the sleigh,
And with her, he rode home.
And when he reached the cottage door,
Oh, how her parents mourned.

The house looked so shut up and empty from outside that I'd expected it to be silent when we walked in, but the whispering hit us as soon as we went through the front door.

"*Let's play the Knife Murder Game . . .*"

"*Yes, yes . . .*"

"*Oh, what fun, what fun!*"

"*Close your eyes and count to ten.*"

"*Who will be the first to die?*"

"*No cheating or peeking.*"

"*Cross your heart and hope to die . . .*"

"*Stick a needle in your eye!*"

I recognized those creepy, giggling voices the moment

I heard them and my heart sank. The Frozen Charlotte dolls were still inside the house. I must have missed some.

From the way Cameron tensed beside me, I could tell that he heard them too. He turned towards me, his face white in the dimness, his eyes wide with disbelief.

"It sounds like they're in the walls," he whispered. "Weren't the ones in the basement plastered into the wall?"

I nodded and we both glanced at the wallpaper in the hall. The dolls must be hidden inside the plaster, nestled into the very foundations of the house.

"What's that smell?" I asked, wrinkling my nose as I suddenly became aware of it.

"It's gasoline."

"Where's it coming from?"

"I don't know."

There was no sign of Piper or Lilias. The staircase that the schoolteacher had broken her neck on all those years ago loomed before us, reaching up into darkness on the first floor. The curtains blocked out the weak sunlight and made it seem like it was the middle of the night. By some unspoken agreement, Cameron and I didn't call out, or turn on the lights, but made straight for the staircase, creeping up it in the dark, hoping that Piper wouldn't know we were there. The whispering followed us all the way up the stairs and I realized that the entire house must be infested with Frozen Charlottes.

Some part of me hoped Lilias would still be locked away in her room, but that hope vanished as soon as we saw her door. It was wide open, and it looked as if Piper had hacked at the lock with her knife.

Guilt twisted in the pit of my stomach. I had told Lilias to lock herself in and then I had left her by herself in the house. Whatever had happened to her, it was my fault.

Cameron stepped into Lilias's room and turned on the light.

Some of her furniture had been shoved up against the door, as if she'd been trying to keep Piper out, but the room itself was empty.

Cameron turned on his heel and came back out to the landing. The expression on his face was so terrifying that I almost took a step back from him.

He drew a deep breath and then shouted out at the top of his voice, "Lilias! Where are you?"

All around us, the hidden Frozen Charlottes giggled and whispered excitedly.

"Where's Lilias?"

"Has anyone seen Lilias?"

"Perhaps she's in the coffin?"

"Perhaps she's in the grave?"

"Perhaps she's all chopped to pieces?"

"Ha! Chopped to pieces!"

Cameron and I raced around the upstairs bedrooms, no longer caring how much noise we made, but there was no sign of Lilias or Piper. Rebecca's room was a terrible mess. It looked like Piper had gone into a rage when she'd seen that the doll cabinet was empty. There was hardly a thing left in the room that hadn't been destroyed. She appeared to have slashed the knife around blindly, demolishing almost everything in sight, including the doll cabinet and the window.

"Insane," Cameron muttered under his breath. "She's finally gone completely insane."

There were even deep gouges in the wallpaper from where she'd dragged the blade along the walls.

We went back to the top of the staircase and, now that the lights were on, I noticed something I hadn't noticed before—there was a drop of blood on the first step. I nudged Cameron and pointed at it. We hurried back down the stairs, noticing more blood every few steps. It led right to the old school hall.

We went straight there and found one light in the huge room already on. It was the spotlight above the stage where Cameron's piano used to be. Lilias stood there by herself with a knife pressed against her neck and tears running down her cheeks.

Cameron stopped dead when he saw her. Slowly, he held both hands out in front of him, palms up, and said in a calm, steady voice, "Lilias, please. Put the knife down."

"The evil skeleton," she whispered. "I can feel the skull grinning inside my head. I don't want it there. I want to cut it out."

"There is no evil skeleton," Cameron said. "Lilias, nothing about you is evil."

"There is. There must be. Otherwise I never could have broken your piano, no matter how many times the dolls told me to."

"I don't care about the piano!" Cameron said. "Do you hear me? I couldn't care less about the piano! The only thing I care about is you. So put the knife down and let's get out of here."

Lilias gave a dry sob and the hand holding the knife trembled. It looked like it could go either way. I didn't dare to breathe. Would she listen to her brother or was she about to cut her own throat right there in front of us?

"Lilias," Cameron said, and his voice was suddenly very quiet, "if you ever loved me at all, even a little bit, you will put down that knife. Right now."

She took a great gasp of air, and the knife fell from her fingers.

In a flash she was off the stage and running to Cameron. Her arms wrapped tightly around his waist and she buried her face in his side.

"Good girl," he said, hugging her back. "Good girl, Lilias!"

The Frozen Charlottes started hissing through the walls.

"Nasty boy!"

"Horrid boy!"

"Always ruins every game!"

"Hateful . . ."

"So hateful . . ."

"Kill him, Piper . . ."

"Pretty, pretty please . . ."

"Do it for us, Piper . . ."

"Put your knife in his heart . . ."

"No, no! Put your knife in his face!"

"Cut out his eyes!"

"And feed them to the cat!"

"Lilias," I said in alarm. "Where is Piper?"

"She's gone," Lilias said. "She said she was going down to the beach to look for the Frozen Charlottes you threw into the sea."

"We'd better check the house," Cameron said, looking at me. "If she really isn't here then we can lock all the doors and keep her out."

I almost didn't hear what he said. One of the big, long windows was uncovered—perhaps Piper had run out of sheets—and for just a brief moment, I thought I saw Rebecca outside the window, her long, dark hair blowing around her, both hands pressed against the glass as she stared at us.

Cameron was already heading for the door with Lilias hanging on to his left hand. I looked back at the window but Rebecca was gone—if she'd ever been there to begin with. Frowning, I hurried after them.

The moment we stepped out of the school hall into the front entrance, the room went completely dark.

Someone had turned off the lights, plunging us into blackness.

I heard Piper shriek as she rushed past me. A blade glinted for just a moment in a chink of light shining in through a gap in the sheets, and then there was a thump and someone grunted in the dark. For a few moments of confusion I didn't know what was going on and, although my hand fumbled for the light switch, I couldn't find it.

Then Cameron's hand closed suddenly around mine, and I knew it was him because I could feel the burnt skin of his scarred right palm.

"Come on," he muttered, already pulling me along, stumbling, behind him.

My free hand found the banister and I realized we were heading up the stairs. I could hear Lilias's footsteps clattering on Cameron's other side and, behind us, Piper was shrieking, "What the *hell* are you doing here, Cameron? You're the only person who could have stopped that brat from slicing herself up once and for all and you're not even supposed to *be* here. You're supposed to be rotting in prison!"

We ignored her and continued up the stairs. The darkness hid us from view and the whispering Frozen Charlottes helped mask our footsteps, but there was nowhere to escape to and it could only be a matter of time before Piper caught up with us. When we reached the landing I thought Cameron would go to one of the bedrooms and try to lock us in but, to my surprise, he headed straight for the end of the corridor instead.

"Where are we going?" I whispered, wishing I could see my way better in the dark.

"The roof," Cameron replied, and the words came out as a gasp. His voice sounded strange, and I knew that something was wrong.

When we reached the end of the corridor, he stopped so suddenly that I bumped into him. My hand came away from his T-shirt slippery and wet.

"Cameron, are you bleeding?" I hissed.

He didn't reply but opened the door and pulled us

through it. A small, steep staircase, almost more of a ladder, led to a trapdoor in the floor. I heard the rusty groan of bolts being drawn back, then Cameron struggling with it, and I put my hands against the door to help. It was incredibly heavy but we managed to push it open and it finally landed back against the floor with a bang. I winced, certain that Piper must have heard it.

"The roof, the roof!"

"They're heading for the roof!"

The Frozen Charlottes whispered in the corridor behind us, and I wished I could smash all their horrid little heads in.

"Go on, Lilias," Cameron said, pushing her up through the trapdoor. It was so narrow that we had to go one at a time.

As soon as Lilias was gone, Cameron's hand was pushing me through. I scrambled out onto the roof beside Lilias. We'd come out onto the flat part with the slate tiles, beside the empty bell tower. The distant roar of the ocean below the cliff seemed to keep in time with the anxious thumping of my heart.

Cameron pulled himself up onto the roof beside us and I saw him stagger as he straightened up. In the evening light I could see what I had felt downstairs—one side of his shirt was soaked in blood, running in a dark stream down his jeans.

"Oh my God, you're hurt!" I said. Lilias whimpered beside me and grabbed hold of my leg.

"I'm all right," Cameron said. "Just help me with this door, quickly, before Piper realizes we're up here!" I rushed to his side and together we gripped the edge of the trapdoor and tried to lift it closed, but it was even harder the other way and, a moment later, I heard Piper screech on the stairs below.

"I'm going to *end* you, Sophie! You should never have touched those dolls! You can't hide behind my brother forever!"

Over the side of the trapdoor I saw her step onto the staircase and jerk her head up to look at us—a weird, snake-like movement that made her appear somehow inhuman. She was still holding the knife and I could see that the blade had blood on it.

Cameron and I strained as hard as we could against the trapdoor. I heard him groan with the effort, but we couldn't quite close it in time and, the next moment, Piper's head appeared at the opening.

I let go of the trapdoor, leaving Cameron to take the full weight, and hurried to the side to kick Piper full in the face before she could pull herself through. I felt savagely pleased by her cry of pain and the series of thumps as she slipped back down the stairs. Served her right for being such a vicious, two-faced witch.

The next second, Cameron managed to slam the door closed. His breath came out in a ragged gasp as he straightened back up. His left hand was clamped to the ripped gash in his shirt, but blood ran down through his fingers and dark spots stained the ground around his feet.

"There's no way to lock the door from this side," he said. "We . . . We have to—" He tried to take a step forward, but his legs buckled beneath him and he fell onto his knees.

Lilias and I both rushed to his side and helped him sit back against the wall. The sight of the wound in his side made me feel light-headed for a moment—it was no mere scrape but a great slash that cut deep. Cameron was shivering, and his hairline was damp with sweat. I knew he was really hurt, and he knew it too, but the look he gave me warned me not to say anything in front of Lilias.

"Here," I said, pulling off my jacket. "Stop the bleeding with this. You'll be fine. It's not . . . It's not bad."

I couldn't help faltering over the blatant lie but Lilias didn't seem to notice as she crouched down by his side, holding on to his hand. And when Cameron's eyes met mine I thought he was grateful to me for trying.

"We need to block the door," he said. "To stop her from coming through."

"You stay there. I'll do it."

But although I searched the roof I couldn't find anything we could use to weigh it down.

"She won't be able to lift it by herself very easily," I said. We all glanced towards the silent door. There'd been no sign of Piper trying to force her way through. Perhaps she didn't fancy getting another kick in the face. "And even if she does manage it she'll need to climb out head first and I can just kick her back down like I did before. She shouldn't be able to reach us up here. We can call the police and just wait her out."

"Have you got your phone?" Cameron asked.

With a sinking feeling I remembered seeing it skitter over the edge of the cliff and fall to the rocks below.

"No, I lost it earlier. On the clifftop. Haven't you got yours?"

Cameron closed his eyes briefly and leaned his head back against the wall. I felt a chill of alarm at how pale he was. "It ran out of battery at the police station," he said.

"Daddy will be back in the morning," Lilias said. "We could just stay up here tonight and wait for him to come home?"

Cameron opened his eyes and looked at me. We both knew he couldn't stay up here on the roof all night. He needed to get to a hospital, and quickly.

"We have to go back," I said. "We have to get out of the house."

"No," Cameron said. "It's too dangerous. We're not going anywhere. She's got a knife, for God's sake."

I shook my head. Lilias and I could wait it out until the morning, but Cameron definitely couldn't.

"You two stay here," I said. "I'll go down and call for help from the landline."

I turned to go back downstairs before Cameron could argue with me but, somehow, he managed to get back to his feet and put his tall body between me and the trapdoor.

"I won't let you go back down there," he said, grabbing my wrist.

"You can't stop me," I replied. Lowering my voice so that Lilias wouldn't hear, I said, "Cameron, you'll die if you stay here."

His grip around my wrist tightened. "Don't you understand?" he said. "This is my fault. I knew that there was something wrong with Piper. I knew she probably had something to do with what happened to Rebecca. I knew and I didn't do anything about it!"

"But what *could* you have done?"

"I don't know . . . Something . . . Anything . . . If you go down there you'll just get yourself killed. At least this way, you and Lilias will survive."

"I'm not going to stand around and watch you sacrifice yourself, if that's what you're asking," I said, shaking him off. "No way. You can forget it. I don't want to hurt you, Cameron, but I *am* going to call for help and you can't stop me."

"What's that smell?" Lilias said suddenly.

"What smell?" Cameron asked.

But I smelled it too and Lilias and I both replied at the same time, "Smoke."

I saw it then, billowing up from the side of the house in a great cloud, swirling with little flecks of ash.

"Oh God," Cameron whispered. "She's set the house on fire."

TWENTY-TWO

Her parents mourned for many a year,
And Charles wept in the gloom.
Till at last her lover died of grief,
And they both lie in one tomb.

For a moment we just stared at each other in horror, trying to work out what to do. Our options seemed pretty limited—either jump from the roof and hope by some miracle not to die, or wait right where we were to slowly burn to death in fiery agony.

"It'll get you this time." Piper's voice floated up to us from the garden. She sounded happy, and I hated her for that. "The fire's come back for you, Cameron, and you won't get away from it again."

I crossed over to the low wall running around the roof and saw Piper standing in the garden, Dark Tom's cage at her feet. She was smiling and, in the light of the flames that were starting to flicker through the windows, she looked like a beautiful, insane devil.

I glanced back at Cameron, alone near the trapdoor, one hand still clamped to his bleeding side, his shoulders hunched, his eyes closed. He looked like someone who had been beaten. Someone who'd been fighting hard for a long time and had finally lost. And I felt a sudden rage come over me, unlike anything I'd ever felt before.

"We are *not* going to die here on this roof!" I said. "We've got to go back through the house. It's our only chance."

I went over to the trapdoor and gripped the handle, putting all my strength into pulling it up. The muscles in my back screamed in protest but I managed to lift the door, causing smoke to billow out onto the roof. I saw Cameron flinch away from it and wondered if the smell reminded him of that day when he'd saved Rebecca from the tree house and burnt his hand in the process.

I thought of that night when I arrived at the house and had smelled something burning and again later when Rebecca had come at me downstairs and I had seen flames that weren't there. Perhaps she had known all along that this was going to happen, perhaps she had seen it somehow and had been trying to warn us.

Some people think spirits can see the future . . . Wasn't that what Jay had said that night at the café?

"How has the fire spread so quickly?" Cameron asked.

"The curtains," Lilias said. "The sheets hanging in the windows. Piper got the gas can from the shed . . ."

I remembered the smell of gasoline when we'd first walked through the front door.

"It's only going to get worse," I said. "We need to go . . . right now."

Cameron held his hand out for Lilias. "Come on. Let's get down from here."

We started to choke on the smoke as soon as we went back inside. Every single room was on fire because of the gasoline-soaked curtains that Piper had hung there. This had clearly been her backup plan all along. The Frozen Charlottes didn't seem so pleased, though.

"Hot," they whimpered inside the walls. *"So hot."*

"It burns . . ."

"Make it stop . . ."

"Piper, please . . ."

"How can you hate them more than you love us?"

"Please, Piper . . ."

We started to make our way back towards the staircase but the smoke snaked down our throats, making it almost impossible to breathe.

I felt Cameron stagger beside me, so I grabbed his arm and draped it around my shoulders. With his body pressed against mine, I could feel the warmth of his blood soaking through my T-shirt and jeans, and I felt sick with worry. When he muttered Rebecca's name I thought he was hallucinating at first, but then I saw her there through the flames. She was standing at the top of the stairs, her lips blue, her hair sparkling with frost, and she was beckoning us towards her.

The three of us hurried forward, trying to ignore the roar of the fire, the crying of the Frozen Charlottes, and the unbearable heat pressing in on us from every angle. The dolls were no longer pleading, but angry instead. I could almost feel their rage burning through the walls as they spat out every swear word I knew, and some I'd never heard of. But there was one word they kept hissing over and over again: *Traitor.*

"Traitorous, traitorous . . ."

"Not going to help us . . ."

"Never really loved us . . ."

"Never . . ."

By the time we reached the top of the stairs, the smoke was so bad that I could barely see a meter in front of my face. I was practically carrying Cameron. My back burned and my shoulders screamed with the effort, and his head kept lolling against my shoulder, so I wasn't sure if he was awake or, I dreaded to think it, even still alive.

I'd lost sight of Rebecca, and the smoke was like a great monster blocking our path. I wasn't sure where the stairs were, and I was terrified of falling all the way down that steep flight and breaking our necks on the bottom like that teacher had done all those years ago.

We're going to burn to death in this house, I thought hopelessly. *Perhaps we should have stayed on the roof after all.*

But then cold fingers curled around mine and I knew that Rebecca was there, even though I couldn't see her through the smoke. I held on to her hand and followed her down the stairs like a blind person.

As she led us through the house I could hear Cameron's labored breathing in my ear and tried to comfort myself with the fact that at least that meant he was still alive. When we got down to the landing, the flames from the rooms on either side seemed to reach out to us like hot, grasping hands, but the cold fingers around mine led us safely straight through the middle to the front door.

We tumbled out onto the porch and the hand suddenly vanished as Rebecca seemed to disappear into the smoke.

As we went down the steps to the garden, I looked at Cameron and my heart turned to ice. Lilias was no longer holding his other hand. She was still back there inside the house. At some point in all the noise and smoke we had lost her.

"Where's Lilias?" I asked.

Cameron looked confused in the firelight, and his eyes struggled to focus on me. "Lilias?" he said, and his voice was slurred. "But . . . isn't she holding your other hand?"

"No! That was Rebecca showing us the way."

"Oh God." Cameron tried to go back to the house but he could barely stand up by himself and it wasn't difficult for me to shove him back into the garden.

"Wait here, I'll find her!" I said.

I ran back up the steps to the front door. As soon as I stepped into the hall I saw Lilias hurrying towards me with Shellycoat clutched to her chest, the old cat covered in ash.

"Come on!" I called. Through the crackle and hiss of the flames I could still hear the Frozen Charlottes snarling and hissing in the walls and the sound sent a chill down my spine. We rushed out of the burning house, taking huge, thankful gasps of the cool sea air outside.

The next few minutes seemed to happen in slow motion. I heard Dark Tom's voice first, squawking from his cage: *"Monstrous!"* he said, just like he had done my first night at the house. *"Monstrous! Monstrous!"*

I turned around and saw Cameron struggling to climb back up the front steps towards us, the sweat running down his face making trails in the ash staining his skin. And Piper was right there behind him, already reaching for him, already grabbing the back of his T-shirt before I had time to scream out a warning.

She yanked him back and he fell onto the grass, his head falling back against the ground with a crack. "You've ruined *everything*!" Piper screamed over him, and in the flickering firelight she no longer looked beautiful, or even pretty. She looked exactly like what she was—a snarling, soul-sucking monster. "I *hate* you, Cameron! I've always hated you!"

She raised the knife and the blade shone silver in the firelight. Cameron tried to prop himself up on one elbow, his good hand stretched out defensively in front of him.

"Piper," he said weakly. "Please . . . don't . . ."

I was running towards them. It felt like I'd been running towards them my whole life. I could hear my own voice screaming at Piper, but it was like moving through tar, and I knew I wouldn't get there in time to stop what was about to happen. All Piper had to do was bring the knife down and it would be over.

But then, just as she was about to do it, her head jerked backward as if she'd been struck. I heard her cry out, and saw the knife fall from her hand to land in the grass as she clutched both hands to her throat.

Blood trickled through her fingers and, with a thrill of horror, I realized it was the necklace.

I could only see the back of the doll's head because its face was turned towards Piper, but I was sure it must be biting her throat because a thin ribbon of blood ran down from it. And the white fingers of all the broken hands were curled into her flesh, as if they were choking her.

"What—" she gasped, clutching at the necklace with both hands.

"Save us."

The dolls' voices poured out of the house over the roar of the fire.

"Forget about them . . ."

"And help us!"

Her hands still clasped to her neck, Piper looked towards the house and, for the first time since I'd known her, I saw fear in her eyes—real, raw, ugly fear.

"But I can't!" she cried. "I can't get you out in time. It's too late!"

"No!"

"We're by the door . . ."

"You can reach us . . ."

"You can . . ."

"You better . . ."

The doll's head at Piper's throat seemed to nuzzle deeper into her neck and blood splattered around it. Piper gave a bubbling shriek and tried to pull the necklace off again, but it was embedded too deeply in her throat, and her fingers tugged at it in vain.

"All right!" I heard her gasp. "All right, I'm coming, I'm coming!"

She half ran, half staggered past us. I didn't know what I could do to help her, or whether I even should, and the next second she'd gone up the porch steps and disappeared into the house.

"Piper," the dolls whispered, *"don't you want to play with us anymore? It's fun to be dead."*

The front door slammed shut behind her and then an explosion of flames broke the downstairs windows into great showers of hot, glittering glass.

"Fire in the hole!" Dark Tom shrieked, frantically flapping his wings in his cage. *"Fire in the hole!"*

Lilias and I ran to Cameron. The knife hadn't touched him but he was lying utterly still in the grass and his eyes were closed, his face too white.

When the lights shone on us I couldn't understand what they were at first. My mind was so numbed by the horror of the last few hours that I didn't realize they were car headlights until Uncle James ran through the gates towards us.

"No, no, no!" he was saying. "Not again, not again!"

"Cameron . . . Cameron's been hurt," I said, and it was an effort to speak—my tongue felt clumsy, my voice sounded strange in my ears. "We need an ambulance."

"It's already on its way," Uncle James said, falling beside Cameron in the grass. "I saw the fire from the road and I knew . . . I knew that Piper had done something again. I heard it in her voice on the phone. That's why I caught the last ferry before they stopped running." Uncle James looked at me and suddenly grabbed my shoulder. "Sophie, you're hurt too!"

I looked down and saw the blood all over my T-shirt and jeans. It was on my hands too, from where I'd helped Cameron out of the house. I shook my head. "It's not mine," I said. I felt so weird, so far away and wobbly. I'd never felt shock like this before, not even when Jay died.

"Lilias, are you okay?" Uncle James said. She was in a heap on the grass, sobbing into Shellycoat's fur. She nodded but couldn't speak.

"It's Cameron. Piper had . . . She had a knife."

Uncle James groaned and turned back to Cameron, leaning over him in the grass. There was so much blood— it shone dark and wet on his clothes and his skin and the ground.

"I should have listened," he muttered, speaking more to himself than to me. "God forgive me, why didn't I listen to him?"

The flashing blue lights signaled the arrival of the fire engine and the ambulance, but Uncle James's face was ashen as he looked up at me in the dancing firelight and, when he spoke, his voice was hoarse. "He's not breathing."

SIX MONTHS LATER

I walked down the street towards the café, the one where it had all started with the Ouija-board app. My coat was buttoned up to my chin and a wool hat was pulled low over my ears. It had snowed earlier in the day and was threatening to do so again. My feet were like blocks of ice in my boots despite the second pair of socks I'd put on.

When I turned the corner into the next street, I saw him right away. He was standing outside the café wearing a blue scarf and a long, dark coat. As I walked down the road, a few flakes of snow began to fall, settling in his black hair. He was gazing around but didn't notice me until I was almost right in front of him—then he broke into a huge smile that made my heart do a kind of flip-flop inside my chest.

I'd worried that it might be a bit weird between us, since we hadn't seen each other in months, but he walked the last few steps to meet me and threw his arms around me in a tight hug. He had to bend his tall body down slightly to my level and I could smell the fresh, minty scent of his shampoo.

Neither one of us spoke for a few moments, and I didn't want the hug to end. It was such a joy to feel the warmth of his body, strong and healthy again, close to mine. It helped to dispel the awful memory of those first few days at the hospital when they hadn't even been sure whether or not he would survive. When the paramedic had revived him at the scene I had been so relieved, but that had just been the start of a long, difficult journey. Now the injury had finally healed, although it had left a jagged scar down his side that he would carry for life.

Eventually, he pulled back and smiled at me. The smile completely transformed his face and brought so much warmth into those blue eyes of his that it was almost like looking at a different person.

"Well," Cameron said. "How are you?"

"Never mind me," I replied, giving him a poke. "Don't keep me in suspense—tell me about your audition!"

"I got in!" he said. "I'll start music school in London in September."

"That's great! Oh, Cameron, I'm so happy for you!"

The snow was coming down even harder now. It felt like we were a million miles away from Skye and last summer and everything that had happened on the island.

"Come on," he said, grabbing my hand. "Let's go inside and get warm."

We ordered hot chocolate and sat down at a table by the window.

"How's Lilias doing?" I asked.

"Really well," Cameron said. "The new house has been so good for her and she's even made friends with the girl who lives next door."

"That's fantastic!"

"And Mom's been doing better too. We've been allowed to see her a couple of times. Since . . . Since Piper died, she seems to have made big leaps in her progress. The doctors are really optimistic about her."

"I'm so glad." I reached across the table and brushed my fingertips against Cameron's hand.

The firemen had gone into the house that night to try to save Piper but, by the time they found her, it was too late. She had burned to death.

"Did you manage to straighten everything out with your parents?" Cameron asked.

"It took a while but they don't think I'm suicidal anymore, if that's what you mean. What happened with the investigation?" I asked. "Into Brett's accident?"

"Officially closed," Cameron replied. "Apparently Piper's friends told the police that Brett . . . well . . ." He suddenly looked apologetic. "That he kissed you that night on the beach."

I could feel myself blushing. "It . . . It's not what you think—" I began, but Cameron instantly put his hand over mine across the table.

"I know," he said. "It's okay. You don't have to explain—I can imagine what happened well enough. I'm only sorry I wasn't there to—Well, anyway, all that matters is that her friends thought that might have given Piper a motive for attacking Brett. And they found her DNA on the needles. But since she's not around anymore . . . well . . . they're not going to charge me with anything. Dad told them about how she set the house on fire and now they're saying that perhaps she had undiagnosed mental problems."

"And the dolls?" I asked quietly. I hesitated to bring them up. Just the mention of them sent a chill through my blood, but I had to know.

"I went back to the house," Cameron said, lowering his voice to match mine. "As soon as they let me out of the hospital, I went back, but it's just a burnt-out shell now. There's nothing left. I combed through the rubble but I couldn't see any Frozen Charlottes. The ones that were left must have all been destroyed when the walls collapsed in the fire."

"So it's definitely over, then."

"It's definitely over," Cameron replied. He leaned back in his chair and looked suddenly nervous as he picked up a menu and fiddled with it. "You'll come and visit me, won't you?" he asked. "When I start school? London's a lot closer than Skye. Or I could visit you, I mean, whatever is—"

"Of course I'll visit," I said, my fingers entwining with his. "All the time."

Cameron smiled at me across the table and just for a moment I almost felt like Jay was there with me too. As if he was glad for me, like he was telling me that it was okay. His voice was clear inside my head. *Be happy, Sophie. That's all I want . . .*

Perhaps Cameron could feel it too somehow, because he said, "Maybe one day we could visit Jay's grave together? I know I never met him but I'd . . . I don't know—I guess I'd just like to pay my respects."

"Of course we can. I think you two would have really liked each other."

Cameron smiled at me and then said, "I'm hungry. Are you hungry?"

"Starving."

He picked up the menu again. "So what's good here?"

I smiled. "Everything."

ABOUT THE AUTHOR

ALEX BELL always wanted to be a writer, but decided to pursue a law degree as a backup plan, writing no fewer than six novels during her time in school. Alex now happily dwells in an entirely make-believe world of blood, madness, and mayhem.